P9-CFL-108

SPARROW

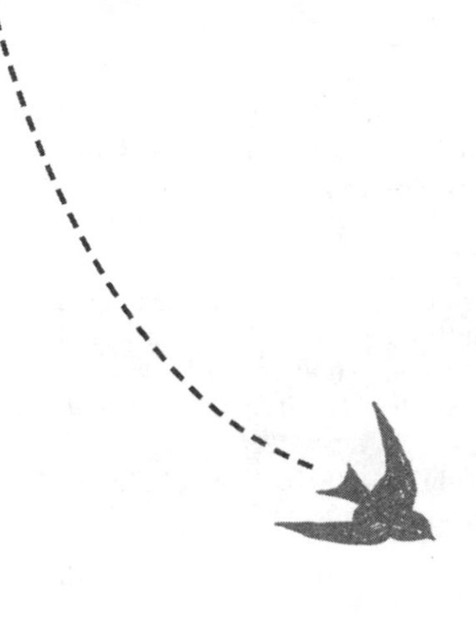

SPARROW

SHERRI L. SMITH

DELACORTE PRESS

Published by Delacorte Press
an imprint of Random House Children's Books
a division of Random House, Inc.
New York

www.randomhouse.com/teens

Educators and librarians, for a variety of teaching tools, visit us at www.randomhouse.com/teachers

Library of Congress Cataloging-in-Publication Data
Smith, Sherri L.
Sparrow / Sherri L. Smith. — 1st ed.
p. cm.
Summary: After the death of the beloved grandmother who raised her, high-school student Kendall Washington travels to New Orleans expecting to be taken in by her only living relative, an aunt, but the reunion does not go as planned.
ISBN-13: 978-0-385-73324-3 (hardcover) —
ISBN-13: 978-0-385-90343-1 (Gibraltar Library Binding)
ISBN-10: 0-385-73324-0 (hardcover) —
ISBN-10: 0-385-90343-X (Gibraltar Library Binding)
[1. Grandmothers—Fiction. 2. Friendship—Fiction. 3. High schools—Fiction. 4. Schools—Fiction. 5. New Orleans (La.)—Fiction.] I. Title.
PZ7.S65932Sp 2006
[Fic]—dc22
2005013654

The text of this book is set in 11.5-point Baskerville.

Book design by Angela Carlino

Printed in the United States of America

10 9 8 7 6 5 4 3 2 1

First Edition

For my grandmother

Prologue

Everybody's wearing black.

Everybody but Mama. She should be wearing her pj's, because Miss Selene says she's sleeping, but it's a special sleep, so she's in her pink dress instead. Daddy's sleeping too, and Mackie. Mackie should take a nap. He's only two. I'm a big girl. I don't have to take one.

"Dear Lord, help this child!" Miss Selene says to Missus Kirkwood. Miss Selene holds my hand real tight. Miss Selene looks after me and Mackie when Mama's working late and Daddy's out of town.

"That child's blessed," Missus Kirkwood says. Missus Kirkwood works with my mama at the bank. That's where they count money. "To walk away from a wreck like that, when her poor family . . . God was watching over her."

"Who is God watching, Miss Selene?" I ask. We are in a church. Mama says church is where God can see all of us.

Miss Selene bends down real low so she's as tall as me. "You, baby girl. God saved you. You must be something special to him."

"Don't go filling that child's head with any more ideas," G'ma says. My g'ma's face is like a crumpled paper bag. She takes my hand from Miss Selene. G'ma's skin feels dry.

Miss Selene turns colors. "I'm sorry, Mrs. Wright. It's a miracle, that's all."

"No miracle in losing three lives," G'ma says.

Miss Selene nods. "Of course, you're right. Kennie is lucky to still have you."

G'ma's voice is loud. "Family is important. I think we'll manage."

Miss Selene doesn't say anything else. She's staring at a lady in the doorway. The lady comes up to us. She's not wearing black. She's wearing purple. G'ma sees her and shakes her head. She must not like purple dresses.

"Mama," the purple lady says.

"Now, you know you don't belong here today," G'ma tells her. "You're two years too late for that."

Miss Selene and Missus Kirkwood look at each other and walk away. I want to go with them, but G'ma's holding my hand.

"Mama, please," the purple lady says. Her face is tight, like a rubber band. "You know I loved Ginnie."

Ginnie is my mama's name. It means Virginia. Daddy calls her Ginnie too.

The purple lady looks at me. "Kennie, do you remember me?"

I scrunch my face up to help me think, but my brain won't let me. I shake my head. The purple lady gets down on her knees. She smells like flowers.

"Last time I saw you, you were one year old. How old are you now?"

I hold up a hand and push down my thumb. "This. And a half."

"Too long . . ." She shakes her head. "Kendall, I'm your aunt Janet. Your mother's sister."

I blink. "Aunt Janet," I say carefully.

The purple lady smiles. She's got Mama's smile. G'ma and Mackie have Mama's smile too. "That's right, Kennie. I've come to take care of you."

"Now, Janet, we've discussed this," G'ma says.

Aunt Janet stands up and fixes her dress. "Mama, I'm her godmother," she says, even though she doesn't look like a fairy.

G'ma shakes her head. "She wouldn't need you to be, if you hadn't been so hardheaded. You should've come back with them, Janet. Gone to college here. Had a chance at a good life. But you turned your back on Virginia, on all of us. And now they're gone. And look at you. You can hardly take care of yourself. What are you going to do with a child?"

Aunt Janet looks angry, the way I am sometimes when Mackie takes my blocks away.

"Mama, I can do this. I've made my own mistakes, but I'll do better with Kendall, for Ginnie's sake."

Now G'ma looks angry too. "Oh, will you?" she says. "Will you feed her? Educate her? With what? You think love is enough to raise this child?"

Aunt Janet sticks her chin out hard. "It would've been enough for me."

G'ma gets her serious voice. It makes me want to let go of her hand.

"Don't sass me, girl," she says. "I raised you two the only way I knew how. At least God gave me one good daughter." G'ma wipes her eyes. "Now he's given me my grandbaby, too. But Janet, before you can take care of anybody, you need to do better with yourself."

Aunt Janet's voice is naptime quiet. "If that's the way you want it," she says. She looks so sad, I want to cry, but I'm a big girl.

"Does Mama know you're here?" I ask. Mama always knows how to make people happy. "She's over there, sleeping." I point to the soft box where she is wearing her pink dress.

Aunt Janet is the one who cries now.

"Your mama knows we're here," G'ma says. "Don't you worry, Kendall, baby. I always told your mother, if anything happened, I'd be here. That's what family does. That's what family's all about."

"Family." I nod. Mama taught me about family. They are always there. They never leave you. Even when they are sleeping.

"Aunt Janet, you're family too, aren't you?" I ask.

Aunt Janet looks at G'ma and looks at me. "Sure, Kennie." She hugs me and kisses my cheek. Her lips feel wet, but I don't wipe it away. "I'm family too." She looks at G'ma again. "Remember that."

Aunt Janet walks away.

"Now, come on, baby girl," my G'ma says. "Let's say goodbye to your mama."

G'ma's being silly. "Goodbye is for when you leave, G'ma. Not for when you go to bed."

G'ma sighs like Mama does when she's tired. I wonder if G'ma needs to take a nap too. "Then come and say good night, Kendall."

And we do.

1

Somebody's singing the blues.

Somebody's feeling like it's the end of the world. Sorrow drowns out the running dish water in the kitchen and the honk of traffic downstairs. If I had the voice for it, I'd sing right along.

I try to follow the thread of music, but G'ma is calling loudly to me.

Today must've been a lonesome day, for her to pull those old records out again. No surprise, cooped up like she's been these past months. And me, I'm not exactly a breath of fresh air. I don't have "young friends" to bring over and "put life" into the place, as G'ma would say. My seventeen's not the ice cream social it was for G'ma in her day. Not since it's just the two of us.

"Kendall, are you listening to me?" she hollers through the kitchen doorway.

"Yes, ma'am." I wash the last of the lunch plates, bits of ham and sandwich spread rinsing down the drain. Of course I'm listening. Everyone in the building's listening to her too. G'ma's not a quiet woman when she's upset.

"You'd better be listening, 'cause your grandmother didn't raise a fool."

I dry my hands and go into the living room to get my coat. G'ma's sitting there on the sofa, waving my report card at me. For a minute, she looks like her old self again, a strong, serious woman, with skin like sweet brown coffee, not dark and bruised-looking like mine. "Cream in my coffee," she used to say to me. " 'Cause my mother wanted me to grow up sweet." They forgot the sugar, I'd want to say to her some days, but she would just shush me up for sassing.

She's got that shushing face on now. Her tough love face. I've seen it more than once since she took me in. And today I've let her down big-time.

"Now, you go right back over to that high school and tell that teacher you want to do extra-credit work, however much it takes, to get your grades back up. My granddaughter is a good student and she's going to graduate with the rest of her class." G'ma swats the sofa arm with my report card, then places it gently down beside her.

I sit across from the sofa on the edge of our old armchair, hands clasped and head down. "Yes, ma'am."

The blues song fades, and another one comes up. I remember the name of this one. It's Sarah Vaughan singing "Misty." *Look at me, I'm as helpless as a kitten up a tree . . .*

"It's only midterms," I say, like that helps. "I know my

science, and English, too. I can get my D up to a B by the end of the semester if I do well on the final."

G'ma takes out a handkerchief and wipes invisible crumbs from her mouth. "Don't put all your eggs in that basket," she warns me. "You were such a good student. Stay that way. I know it's been difficult, but don't let this"–she waves her hand in the air–"don't let this stop you."

"This" means G'ma. We don't talk about it much, but we both know the stroke she had last summer hurt her more than a little. The afghan over her lap reminds me that her legs aren't what they used to be. Winter doesn't help either, especially not the icy winter Chicago gets. We keep up the exercises the doctor gave her, and they help. She's walking with a cane now. But we live on the second floor of a brownstone walk-up, and the kitchen is a long twenty steps from the sofa. So I come home at lunch and straight after school. I help her walk to the bathroom, I make dinner, breakfast, and lunch. If that means leaving English a little early, or getting to chemistry a little late, so be it. I owe G'ma more than a few skipped classes. Besides, I feel better when I'm around.

After a minute, G'ma lets me stand up.

"Lunch was okay?" I ask, grabbing my coat from the chair by the door. The smell of fried ham still hangs in the air. I boil it first, to get the salt out. G'ma likes her ham on white with mayonnaise, but she doesn't seem to mind the low-fat spread I've been using instead. The doctors say anything I can do to lower her cholesterol will reduce the likelihood of another stroke.

"Very tasty," G'ma says. "Just leave me a little water before you go. And cut off that phonograph player."

Phonograph player. I shake my head and cut off the turntable. For all her talk of the future, G'ma has some old-fashioned ways about her that baffle me. She'd fight me tooth and nail before she'd ever let me play her a CD, and forget about a cell phone–even if we could afford one on her pension.

"Here you go." I set down a fresh glass of water on the coffee table in front of her and kiss her papery cheek. "See you later."

"Be good. And tell that teacher what I said." She pats me on the shoulder. I turn the TV on to her talk shows and head out into the Chicago wind.

— — —

"Kendall, I don't know what to tell you. There's only so much extra credit you can do without lab work." My chemistry teacher frowns at me through her square glasses and taps a pen on the lab table. Ms. Hansen has a smoker's voice and a thing for wearing her ex-husband's sport jackets. She calls them her alimony. "AP Chem is hard work." She shakes her head and sighs. "You have to show up for the labs."

"I know." I nod. "But the insurance only pays for nurse visits, not day care. I don't know what else to do."

Ms. Hansen gives me a long look that might be sympathy but makes me remember I haven't touched a hot comb to my hair in days. With the ponytail holders I shoved in this morning, I must look like a poodle. I don't even want to know what I looked like yesterday.

She shakes her head, her own crazy gray curls bouncing around her shoulders. "Tell you what. We'll make this work. You do two papers for me and get at least a B on the final, and I think you'll be all right."

"Okay," I agree, relieved. "Thank you."

She smiles, and I get a faint whiff of cigarette smoke. "Don't thank me. Just get the job done."

"Yes, ma'am."

— — —

It's too early for rush hour, but traffic noise is already bouncing off the walls outside the school when I leave. The campus has mostly cleared out–talking to Ms. Hansen took a while. But the cool kids are still here, the ones that don't need to take a bus or catch the L, the elevated train. The ones lucky enough to have their own cars.

I duck my head down as I pass the student parking lot. It's half the size of the one for teachers because most kids don't use it. The handful that do are standing around, leaning up against their rides–a mix of new cheap cars and old vintage deals. The girls are all lean and pretty, and the boys are all jocks or rock stars. Definitely not my crowd.

"Hey. Kendall."

I almost choke on my own tongue, hearing my name coming from one of them. I look up and the wind bites my cheeks, tugging water from the corners of my eyes.

Hannah Lee is peeling herself away from the group and coming toward me. She's wearing a boy's coat over her unreasonably short cardigan and even shorter skirt. I don't remember her legs being quite so long. It must be the tights. I feel like a snowman in my winter coat and bushy hair.

"Hey," Hannah says again. This time, she gives a little wave to catch my attention. Like seeing my best friend from a former life actually acknowledging me wouldn't be enough. I stop in my tracks.

"Boy, private school agrees with you," I say by way of hello. And it does. I take her in, the long shiny hair with a newly dyed streak of auburn at the brow and the *Seventeen* magazine lip gloss. I recognize the face, almond eyes, almond skin, but she's light-years away from the pudgy little girl I knew in grade school.

"Yeah, I guess," she says, pulling a strand of hair out of her shiny mouth. "But it's a drag, too. All the cute boys are at your school." She giggles, and it's so much more girly than she sounded our sophomore year, before her parents decided they could afford to go private. I shake away the thought of what it would have been like to still have her around.

"What about you?" she asks.

I shrug. My coat feels uncomfortably hot. "You know, fine, I guess."

"How's your grandma?"

"Good. Better. She was sick over the summer, but she's doing great now." A flicker of concern crosses Hannah's face. But I shrug it off. "No, we're fine."

"Okay. That's good."

We both shift from foot to foot. The car kids are probably staring at us. Seeing old friends shouldn't make you feel so alone.

She twists the reddish streak of hair around her finger. "What do you think? Very un-Korean, eh?"

I smile a little. Before she became Miss Glamour Teen USA, Hannah was the standard first-generation American daughter of Korean immigrants. Back in grade school, she was quiet, with black hair down to her butt, and with all the filial piety/parental obedience junk heaped on her shoulders. Hannah was destined to take care of her parents the way I've been watching after G'ma. At least, that's what she used to tell me.

Looks like she found a way to buck the system.

"Your parents must've freaked."

Hannah gives me an impish look. "Not as much as when my mom saw this." She lifts up her sweater and flashes a belly-button ring. I almost pass out.

"No way."

Hannah nods. "Way. Jimmy likes it. And I do too. I swear, it just got so boring being their little girl all the time. So, whatever, you know?"

"Yeah," I say, but I don't know. I don't own any lip gloss, and my hair is . . . well, my hair.

"Do you know Jimmy? Jimmy Pritchard? He's in your year." I shake my head.

She smiles shyly. "Yeah, well. We're together. He's taking me bowling up on Sheffield for my birthday. Maybe you could come."

Like a slide show in my head, I remember that bowling alley from the second grade. Hannah's seventh birthday. Timmy Long kissing me. My first kiss. Pretty much my last, too.

"What ever happened to Timmy Long?" I ask without meaning to. Hannah smiles. For a second, I feel like we could be those two little kids again, giggling and scheming behind our pink polished fingers, done up especially for that day.

"He was dating that skank Hilary, from eighth grade, remember? And then they broke up when his folks moved. Wisconsin, I think. We don't keep in touch."

"Yeah, neither do we."

We shift a little uncomfortably, the quick intimacy gone as fast as it had come.

"I miss you, Kennie."

"I miss you, too. . . . Hannah Bobana."

Hannah smiles again, and I see that the braces did their work. I can't believe it, but I'm jealous of this girl, who used to be like a sister to me.

"Hey, look, I've got to go catch my ride. But I hope you can come."

"Yeah." I nod. "I'd like that."

"Good, good. Okay, um, wear something cute. It's Saturday night at seven."

"Cool." I wave goodbye and watch Hannah's "ride" drive up–a guy in an old apple green Porsche. That must be Jimmy. Their liplock makes it obvious.

Wow. Hannah's got a boyfriend. I look down at my faded jeans with the leggings showing through the hole in the knee, and my baggy sweater. Wear something cute, she says. That's a shopping trip, for sure.

A bus goes by me, kicking up a cloud of black smoke. I hold my breath and race home to share the double news of seeing Hannah and getting a second chance at chemistry.

Outside the apartment, I fumble for my key, but the door is already open.

"Hello?" G'ma doesn't answer.

"Hello?"

"Aiee, Kendall," Mrs. Alonso from next door calls to me from her doorway. She's in that same old ratty pinstriped housedress, the slippers coming off her feet, curlers permanently anchored in her hair. Her face looks soft and sad.

"Where's my grandmother?" I snap at her, and feel bad for it.

"The ambulance take her away. I think she broke her hip or something. I hear her fall through the air vents." She points overhead. "Boom! And then she was calling your name. So I call the police. I don't have a key to get in, and I knew she needed help."

"Where is she?" My skin's crawling right off me.

"Grant Memorial."

"Thank you." I squeeze her hand and run.

2

There's too much quiet in this room. Outside, folks are walking, shoes squeaking on the pine-scented linoleum, intercom blaring. But in here, it's just me, the doctor, and silence. I can't stand it.

When the doctor clears his throat, I just about scream.

"Not broken, just bruised," he says. He's reading from an X-ray of G'ma's hip. Still in one piece, thank God, thank God. While I was busy chatting it up with Hannah, G'ma got up to get another glass of water and lost her balance. An accident, nothing more. "She'll have to stay with us a few days," the doctor adds.

"But she's okay?" My heart feels stuck. It didn't race when I ran the ten blocks to get here. I can't feel it beating now. This doctor, with his clean coat and name tag, I bet his heart has never stopped beating, like mine.

"To tell the truth, we'd like to do a few tests. It's possible she had another minor episode."

"Episode?" Like she's some kind of TV show. "What do you mean? Another stroke?" I feel panic rising in me again. The first stroke changed everything. It can't happen again, or it'll only be worse.

The doctor bounces his clipboard against his thigh. It makes me want to break that board over his head, but when he speaks, he sounds genuinely concerned for me. "It's always a possibility. Having already had a stroke increases the chance of it happening again. But let's see what the tests say. Your grandmother's a strong woman, Miss Washington. Strong-willed, too." He smiles a little and I start to breathe again. If she's causing trouble, I know she's okay.

"Can I see her?"

"She should be in her room by now. Check with the nurses' station next door."

"Thanks." I turn to go, but now my runner's legs are like rubber. I take a deep breath. Around the corner, the nurses are nice. They give me sympathetic smiles and point the way to G'ma's room.

G'ma's in a huff when I get there. G'ma never was a small woman, but to me, she looks like a bag of bones beneath all that meat and skin. Like she's shriveling up on the inside, a bird in an egg. Her skin looks ashy and her face is pinched tight.

"Kendall Washington, where have you been? Men coming all up in the house and hustling me off. I've been calling for you all afternoon."

There's no point in arguing. "Mrs. Alonso told me where you were."

I go up to G'ma and give her a hug. She's in a pale green hospital gown, not the navy blue cardigan I left her in. Worse than that, she doesn't have her wig on. Her white hair sticks up all over the place. She'd be mad if she knew.

"Doctor says you'll be okay." I kiss her cheek. G'ma shakes her head.

"This old hip of mine won't get the best of me."

I squeeze her hand. G'ma was just getting her strength back enough to go outside again. But Chicago winters and a bad hip don't go too well together. Tears start to sting my eyes.

"I'm sorry, G'ma."

"Child, what are you sorry for?" She shakes my hand like it'll shake away the sorrow, then she pats the bedspread with her palm. I sit beside her.

"I ran into Hannah Lee after school. If I hadn't stopped to talk to her . . ."

"Oh, hush," G'ma says. "I haven't heard that name in a month of Sundays. It's good for you to have friends."

"I guess."

"You guess. Well, I *know*. Family's important, baby, but friends are too. Now, go call that nurse for me and tell her you're going to get my things. If I'm here for more than a day, I'm gonna want my own nightgown and slippers, you hear? It'll help me sleep right."

I feel numb. "I just got here." I want to stay, to hug her, to know she's all right.

"The sooner you go, the sooner you'll get back," she says.

Suddenly, I'm so tired, I could lie down and die. But then who would get G'ma's nightgown? I hold in a sigh and stand up.

"I'll be back." I wake up my old rubber legs and walk out into the hallway. At least G'ma will be in someone else's hands for a while. Maybe I can get some sleep now, without taking her to the bathroom at all hours of the night. Maybe I can get my extra homework done.

Kendall, you'll go to hell for thinking like that, I tell myself. When I get home, I'll pack two bags. There's no way I'm leaving G'ma alone in this place if I don't have to.

— — —

I spend an hour trying to find G'ma's wig. I swear that thing's got a life of its own. Can't blame it for not wanting to sit on her old hard head all day, though. I give Mrs. Alonso the news about G'ma's hospital stay, and head back to Grant.

It's late by the time I get there. G'ma's already asleep in that paper robe they gave her. So much for the nightgown.

I set down her bag and watch her sleep. G'ma. Sometimes I can see my whole family in her face. There's Mama's mouth, pulled into that little frown, and Mackie's bump of a nose. I memorized every inch of my family's snapshots after they died, till G'ma said I'd wear the pictures out. I even used to sit in front of the bathroom mirror and smile, smile, smile. But I never really looked like Mama. G'ma did, though. And she promised me she wouldn't wear out anytime soon.

I turn away from the hospital bed and stare out the window. It's getting dark outside, and the temperature's dropping. I press my hand to the glass and let it get cold. It's warm in the hospital, warmer than it ever gets at our place. G'ma's room is a semiprivate. That means there's a second bed in the room with a curtain between them. That bed's empty right now. I'm tempted to use it. Instead, I sit in the guest chair and turn the TV down low. The news is on when I fall asleep.

"Excuse me, miss." A nurse is staring me in the face. She's round everywhere, with big brown eyes and a big brown face. "Visiting hours." She taps her watch.

"Sorry." I get up. "They let me stay with her last time. I don't feel right leaving her alone here."

The nurse nods. "They'll let you do that in intensive care sometimes, but believe me, your grandmother's in good shape. She'll be all right with us."

I frown. Lord knows I want to sleep in a bed tonight, not a chair. But G'ma . . .

"Listen," the nurse says, reading my mind. "My name is Charlotte. I'll be on duty until ten. If anything happens before then, I'll give you a call. And I'll make sure the other nurses do the same. The best thing you can do right now is get yourself a good night's sleep."

"You're right," I agree, although I think I just wanted her permission to go. I unfold myself from my chair and grab my travel bag. "I brought my grandmother's nightgown. It's in the closet, if she wants to put it on."

"Will do." Charlotte nods.

"I'll see you at lunch tomorrow, G'ma." I kiss her cheek. She murmurs in her sleep.

"Bye, now," the nurse says. It's nine o'clock, and it's gotten colder. I leave G'ma at the hospital and walk the ten frozen blocks home.

— — —

"Kendall? Kennnndaaaall!"

"I'm comin'," I mumble, and trip over my overnight bag jumping off the couch. Must've been sound asleep, but that woman's voice could wake the dead.

"Right here, G'ma," I call out, staggering into her bedroom. "Just asleep on the sofa. Whatchyou need?"

I turn on the light.

The bedroom's empty. I sag against the doorway. I'm hearing things. G'ma's in the hospital calling some nurse for help to the bathroom, not here, calling out to me. I'm a basket case. I feel embarrassed even though I'm alone. "Good night, G'ma," I say softly, and drag myself off to my own bed.

This morning, the halls of the hospital smell like rubbing alcohol. They must've run out of pine cleaner during the night. The floors are so shiny, they make my shoes squeak. It's eleven a.m. I meant to be here at nine, when visiting hours start, but I overslept. There's a nurse in G'ma's room, standing by the bed when I come in.

"There she is!" It's Charlotte, the nurse from last night. G'ma's wide awake, but she doesn't take her eyes off the television. "Grandbaby Kendall, you want to give a try at feeding your grandmother here?" She's polite, but I know she's had it. G'ma hates hospital food. She won't touch it. Too bland. But I've got hot sauce in my bag. If the nurse leaves, she'll choke down what I give her.

"Thank you." I nod to Charlotte and drop my bag on the guest chair.

"Enjoy your lunch, Mrs. Wright," Charlotte says to G'ma. Her voice is so happy, I can't tell if she's being sarcastic. "I'll just leave you two alone," she says, and rushes out the door.

"Hey, G'ma." I give her a kiss on the cheek and take a look at the lunch tray. "Looks like salisbury steak again." Salisbury steak, a specialty of the house that I had more than my share of last summer.

"Don't want none." G'ma's watching that old talk show again. I know she's not really listening; the sound's down too low. But she likes to watch the people move across the screen. Like her own private movie, and she makes up the words.

"Here." I pull out the hot sauce and dump it all over her plate until the mashed potatoes look orange and the little lump of ground beef is swimming in reddish brown gravy.

G'ma sniffs the air. She looks sideways at the plate and tries hard not to smile. Her hand comes away from her face, where she'd been resting her head, and she nods the okay for me to give her a forkful. I do, and she eats quietly. She's forgotten to put her dentures in again, and her mouth makes soft smacking noises.

"G'ma, I still can't find your wig, but you need to do something about that hair." It's a ruin of gray and white knots. She used to keep it in an old sixties kind of bouffant before it got too hard to keep up. Then she got the wig. Now she's just letting it go.

"Why don't you braid it for me, baby."

"I'd break a comb trying." She stops eating and cuts me a look. I search the nightstand for a comb.

"Don't blame me if you're tender-headed," I warn her, and tackle the mess on her head.

We lose three teeth on the comb, but I'm able to weed them out of her hair, and eventually she looks presentable.

"Now," G'ma says, and swats my hands away. "Get me some water and talk to me."

I pour from the little plastic pitcher on her nightstand. "I talked to my chemistry teacher. She's letting me do the extra credit. I've got papers to write, and I need to get into the lab at some point, but I think I can work it out."

G'ma claps her hand on my knee. "All right, now. That's what I wanted to hear! Back on track in school. That's a good thing, Kendall. When I get myself out of here, we'll celebrate. We'll get ourselves a cab, go pray at the altar, and afterwards, I'm taking you to the Original House of Flapjacks. I'm gonna get that big old Dutch pancake they make, and you can have the waffles with ice cream and strawberries. How's that sound to you?"

I'm already smiling. "You know it sounds good."

The Original House of Flapjacks is an IHOP rip-off that's even better than the real thing, if you ask me. They make these gigantic deep brown Dutch pancakes that rise up in a skillet like a cake, then pop and sink back down into the pan. Dust them with powdered sugar and a squitch of lemon, and you're all set. G'ma loves them. Mama did too. Me, I'm more into sugar than that. The waffles and ice cream come on a plate as big as my head with the hair combed out.

"We haven't been there in a long time," I say. Sunday brunch at our house looks like Aunt Jemima or Bisquick cakes, and instant grits on the side. G'ma thinks they're the best. But grits are nasty, even with butter in the middle.

"Yes, indeed," G'ma's singing. "Dutch pancakes and sweet black coffee. When they check me out, make sure you bring my hat. We are going to church, and you are going to graduate like you're supposed to. Now, what time is it? You'd better get to class before you start that mess all over again."

"Yes, ma'am." I kiss her cheek and try not to let her know I already missed half a day. I don't know why it is, but the sleep you lose the night before always catches up in the morning. At least today G'ma's looking good. I feel my worry start to ease up enough to get me through the day, and hopefully the night, too.

— — —

The house is empty and I've got homework to do. G'ma told me not to come to the hospital today until I was done. That gives me three hours before visiting doors close. I try to get to it, but my heart's slowing me down.

Hannah's bowling party is in two days. With everything that's happened, I'd almost forgotten it. Now it's giving me this twisting feeling in my gut. I can't go out partying with G'ma in the hospital. She might need me. And if she comes home, I know she'll need me then. Not to mention the "wear something cute" rule, and all the extra chemistry work. I guess that's why Hannah's the one with the lip gloss and the boyfriend. I've got other things on my mind.

The house feels empty. I want my G'ma to come home.

Normally, she'd be here, talking to me the whole time. Or asking me to make lunch or turn the TV on. It's off now. The only show I like to watch is reruns of *Mary Tyler Moore,* but she's not on until after eleven.

This is what G'ma sits through every day. No wonder she's so chatty when I get home.

I stare at my science book harder. After a minute of reading the same line again and again, I get up and walk the five steps to the record player.

"Let's see." I shuffle through the stack G'ma left on top of the turntable cover before I realize the record she was listening to yesterday is still on the player. I turn it on. G'ma's lonesome day music fills the room and suddenly, it's not so empty. The blues sound brighter to me today. I hum along, slowly at first, haltingly. And then I fall into my reading, the music swelling behind me. G'ma's not here, but her music is the next best thing.

"Why should I be discouraged . . . ?" I sing along, the formulas on the page in front of me whirling into shapes I recognize. "When trust I have in Thee? His eye is on the sparrow, and I know He watches me."

It's some old song, not really blues, more like a spiritual, a gospel hymn, except for the way the old guy's singing it to his guitar. They played this song at my family's funeral. It was the song on my mother's old jewelry box, one of those musical things that tinkles out sappy songs. I played that little box until it broke, only six months after the funeral. I wish I had kept it, the way G'ma keeps these records. But I was a kid; I didn't know any better. This was before the photo album fixation, and G'ma was so worried about me, she didn't take it away. But once it broke, she took the music box in one hand and my face in the other.

"That'll be enough, now," she said to me. Which meant no more playing the music box, no more thinking I was any more or less special than anybody else. No more thinking that Mama was gonna come back through that door.

A tear falls on page 230 of my science book. I shake my head, wipe my eyes, and close the book over my fingers.

The phone rings. I must've been on the prayer hotline, because when I answer, it's the hospital. They're discharging G'ma in the morning. She's coming home.

3

In the three whole days G'ma has been in the hospital, I've been so wrapped up with worry and lack of sleep that I only did one extra lab experiment, and wrote half an outline for extra credit. She'd be ashamed of me if she knew. I'm not going to let her be. Today I get to working so hard and doing so well that I miss visiting hours before I know it.

G'ma never answers the phone in her room, so I call the nurses' station on her floor and ask them to tell her I'll be there to get her in the morning. I'm catching up. Tomorrow's Friday, but that's G'ma's day. I can turn my schoolwork in on Monday and then I'm done.

I crawl into my bed and sleep like a newborn. G'ma'll be here in the morning. I want to wake up on the right side of my own bed, not the sofa, for once.

The phone wakes me before my alarm clock gets the chance.

"May I speak to Kendall Washington?"

"What? Yes." I'm slurring, I'm so sleepy. "This is she."

"Uh, this is Charlotte, from Grant Memorial? I told you I'd call if anything happened."

"Yeah?" I wait, my head full of cotton, not understanding.

"Your grandmother's had another stroke."

The words sink in slowly, like a ship going down into icy waters. "Thank . . . thank you." I hang up.

I pull on my jeans, my sweater, still on the floor by my bed. I kick my homework across the room trying to get my shoes on faster. I'm all thumbs and dead limbs. My head is ringing, like a gun went off in my ears. The traffic outside sounds far away, and there's only ringing, ringing as I run to the hospital, coat half on, shoes undone. This can't be right. This can't be right. This can't be right.

But it is.

I push past the nurses at the doorway. G'ma's lying on the bed, bathed in yellow light. I can't see where it's coming from, but it's right on top of her, and I know she's going to die.

"G'ma–" The doctor steps back. He lets me in beside her. G'ma looks like she's struggling, gasping for air, like a swimmer after being too long in the sea. A long hollow sound is coming from her throat. She's calling out. Calling for me.

"G'ma . . . ," I say to her again. She takes my hand, clutches it hard, and stops straining for breath. She looks me full in the eyes and relaxes.

"Baby girl," she whispers, and it's as slurred as my own

sleepy words were. Worse, because her right side doesn't move when her mouth does. She's paralyzed. "I'm sorry, Janet, I'm sorry," she mumbles over and over again.

"G'ma?" I start to cry. She's got nothing to be sorry for.

"Forgive me." G'ma closes her eyes. When they open, she's not looking at me anymore. She's looking at something between us. I squeeze her hand.

"G'ma. It's me, it's Kendall."

"Kennie," she says, and grips my hand hard. A nurse runs to get the chaplain. Oh, God.

"Please," I whisper. "No."

Her eyes don't look right. They're cloudy, almost blue. "No, don't leave me." I scream the words, but my throat's so tight, they come out as a whisper. "No." I climb onto the bed, hugging G'ma to me. She's so small, so light, even though she's my big, strong grandmother. "Oh, God." Her grip on my hand is slipping. She's getting heavy, too heavy to hold.

"Don't leave me." I pray. But it's not enough. She's gone.

The chaplain comes too late for absolution. He says a blessing, and the nurses try to pull me away. They aren't strong enough. Nothing can move me. G'ma is my family. My family. She can't go on without me. She wouldn't. She won't.

4

They give me a sedative so I can stop the dry heaves that are doubling me over. I barely keep it down. I should have been there. I should have put away my schoolwork and seen G'ma. I should've never stopped to talk to Hannah. Now it's too late. Everything's too late.

The drug sets in slow and heavy. I feel the room start to fade away. It's like my body's packed in cotton. I can see the nurses, the doctor, G'ma. But I'm going completely numb.

The chaplain suggests they give me time alone with G'ma to say goodbye. I sit with G'ma for a couple of minutes that feel like hours, so stuffed with sedatives and disbelief that I'm almost completely calm when they come to take her away.

G'ma's nurse, Charlotte, says the hospital social worker can help me make funeral arrangements.

But G'ma already handled that. I look at the nurse through damp eyelashes. Her mouth twists in concern and she gives me another pill.

"I wouldn't, usually," she says, "but it'll help you sleep. The social worker will call Child Services to check up on you after you've gotten some rest. Take care of yourself, Miss Washington."

I nod to say thank you, although I don't feel grateful, or worried. Just numb.

Charlotte offers to get me a cab. The clock on the wall says it's 2:00 a.m., but I turn it down. Not a soul passes me on the cold walk home.

– – –

I wake up in my own bed nine hours later, the second Percocet still cottoning up my head. I lie there for a full minute listening for G'ma before I remember. Now I don't want to move. If I move, it means she's really gone. But my head won't let me sleep.

There's a sheet of paper in the top drawer of the kitchen counter with three numbers on it–my school, G'ma's doctor, and Gravenstein Brothers Mortuary. They handled my parents and Mackie when I was little, and they've even got a place there for me, one day. Today, they'll take care of G'ma.

The man on the phone says he'll handle everything. They'll send a car around to the hospital for "the remains," as he puts it, and he'll set up a time for the service in their little chapel. He asks for information about G'ma to put in the paper.

"I don't know . . . um, Louisa Ella Wright, mother–"

"Beloved mother."

"And grandmother."

"Yes, survived by?"

Survived by. Like G'ma was some kind of accident to walk away from. "Me . . . I guess." If this is surviving. I feel like a cigarette, all burnt to ash.

"Services will be at two o'clock on Tuesday. We'll run it in the paper. Is there any other family to notify? Friends?"

"Uh . . . the church, I guess." I remember them reading the names of the deceased at the end of the sermons some days. "But we haven't been there in . . . months."

"Yes. Well, try to let the pastor know. He'll spread the word."

That one almost makes me laugh. That's what pastors are supposed to do. Spread the Word. In addition to making you slow down, Percocet must make you punchy, too.

"Okay," I say.

"And what about your aunt?"

"What?" I feel like I've got clouds in my head. I sit down on the arm of the sofa. "I don't have an aunt."

The undertaker clears his throat. "Well, when your grandmother made arrangements for herself and your family, a Janet Wright was included in the family plot."

I sit there, the phone in my hand. Janet. G'ma's last words. *Forgive me.* "I'm sorry. I don't understand."

"Mrs. Wright had two daughters. Your mother, Virginia, and Janet. I assume she'll want to be at the service."

"There must be a mistake. I . . . I don't have an aunt." G'ma would have told me, otherwise. Family was everything to her.

"Miss Washington?" the undertaker says.

"Yes?"

"Don't worry. Everything will be fine."

"Okay." I hold on to his promise and my Percocet buzz as I hang up the phone. Janet Wright. G'ma was calling out to someone, but a daughter? It just can't be.

At one o'clock, the man from the funeral home comes to pick up G'ma's burial clothes. I give him the periwinkle dress and the Sunday hat she was supposed to wear to breakfast, and some jewelry. She'll get to wear them in church after all.

I'll buy her a new wig, I decide. She'd want that at least. As for the rest of her stuff . . . I don't know what to do with it. G'ma would've told me what to keep.

The man takes what I give him, and jogs back down the stairwell. I follow him out and I stand on the front steps to watch him drive his big old funeral home car away. I wish he'd take me with them. With everyone in my family gone, I'm just remains too.

— — —

I head back upstairs, only to find Mrs. Alonso standing in the doorway, hands clutched like she's praying.

"I'm so sorry, *hijalita*. She was a good lady."

There's a bell ringing in my head, one loud note. Not a school bell or an alarm clock, but a church bell, loud and deep-down lonely. Mrs. Alonso shuffles in her slippers, like she might let me in, but in the end she says, "If there's anything I can do . . ." and shuts the door. Neighbors are just neighbors, after all. Not like they're family.

Family. I go back inside the apartment. It doesn't feel like a home anymore. As I lock the door, I realize today is Hannah Lee's birthday. Right now she's in her lip gloss and tights, bowling up on Sheffield with Jimmy. I hiccup down a sob.

I sit down on the couch and cover my head with a pillow.

I don't have an aunt. I don't.

And then I remember, slow like the way fluorescent lights come on in homeroom after a long weekend break. Another woman, in purple, at a funeral long ago. My family's funeral.

The purple lady leans down to me. Suddenly, I know who Janet is. And I'm not so alone.

"I'm your aunt Janet," she says. Janet Wright. Virginia's sister. G'ma's other daughter.

I find her letter in the bottom of a shoe box in the way top of the hallway closet. I remember G'ma putting my mother's things in here a long time ago. I'm coming down from my Percocet high, but I still feel light-headed.

"Dear Ginny," the letter says. "Please understand when I say I just had to get away." I scan the rest of the page. It's signed "Love, Janet." It's the only one in the box, but that's all I need. There's an address on it, in New Orleans. I get on the phone and dial information.

"What city, please?"

"New Orleans."

"What listing?"

"Janet Wright."

"Please hold while I look up that number."

Holding lasts forever. And then: "The number you've requested is–" I drop the pen I'm writing with and fumble to pick it up again. The number repeats. My heart bounces in my chest like a rubber ball.

I dial.

"Hello?" a woman answers. She's got that same lilt G'ma's voice had, but deeper.

"Hello . . . hi. . . . May I speak to Janet Wright, please?"

"Who's this?"

"Is this Janet?"

"Who's this?"

"Uh . . . I'm . . . this is Kendall . . . Washington. Virginia's daughter."

"Ginny?" There's a long silence. "Kendall, baby, how are you?"

"Aunt Janet?" Thank God, thank God. I feel the blood come back to my face. "Aunt Janet, I'm so sorry. G'ma passed away today. She died at the hospital. She was supposed to be coming home. It was a stroke. She . . . the funeral's Tuesday. You've gotta come. You've got to."

This time, the quiet is so heavy, I think I've been cut off. I feel hot and cold at once. I'm going to pass out if she doesn't answer me.

Suddenly, she breathes out a deep sigh. "Mama."

"I know." It hits me. "Oh no." My face is wet, my eyes hot. I start to feel sick again. Hollow. "So . . . so, the service, it's Tuesday. Can you come? Please come."

"Of course, Kennie. Poor baby. Of course I'll be there. You shouldn't have to handle this alone. Family is family."

My knees give out and I end up on the floor.

"Baby, shhh," she tells me. Eventually, I'm able to give her the address of our apartment, and the funeral home.

"Two o'clock." I'm not alone.

"I'll be there, baby. Now hush, and try to get some sleep."

I won't need that second Percocet tonight. I don't even worry when the phone rings and it's the hospital social worker, checking up on me. Child Services will follow up, she says, but it doesn't matter. Aunt Janet is coming. I promise that we'll set up an interview with a caseworker as soon as we can.

Everything will be all right. Family's coming. That's all the comfort I need.

5

Everybody's wearing black. Everybody except for me.

I'm wearing purple. Purple corduroy pants that are too tight, and a black blouse with a purple sweater. They're the only decent dark clothes I have. I feel bad because G'ma would hate it. She'd say, "Never wear purple at funerals. Purple is a carnival color. Black shows respect." I take off the sweater, even though it's chilly in here, and hope that the black shirt is enough.

The preacher's here, and Mrs. Alonso, and there are about ten people behind me on either side. A couple of faces from the church, but nobody that really knows me or G'ma. That's what real church people are like, G'ma told me once. They show up when no one else does.

I should have called Hannah Lee, but it was just too

weird. Still, it would've been nice to have a friend with me. Even a "used to be" friend like Hannah.

I'm sitting in the front row of the church, the family pew. G'ma's here too, of course, lying in that box up front. G'ma's surrounded by calla lilies. She doesn't look like herself today. Mama's mouth, Mackie's nose, I can't see them anymore. No, that's someone else in G'ma's periwinkle dress and matching hat.

"Miss Washington." The pastor's a big man with a deep voice and sad eyes. He touches my shoulder. "We've got to begin. I'm sorry."

"It's okay." I nod, and clutch a pew Bible in my hands. Two days isn't a lot of time to get from New Orleans to Chicago. The bus takes almost that long. So does the train. Aunt Janet could've flown in. I would've if it was me. But that's money, too. Maybe she'll come tomorrow.

The preacher says a bunch of things about G'ma, most of them true. She was a good woman. She loved her family, and her church family too. She suffered when Mama, Daddy, and Mackie died. He also says she was blessed to have me, and asks everyone to help me in this difficult time, the way family would. But family doesn't just pat your hand and say they're sorry. Family doesn't press ten dollars into your fist and hope to see you next Sunday.

After the service and the burial, the preacher gives me his home number and says, "If there's anything at all I can do." I nod, and agree that I'll finish school. That I'll come to church. It's three months until I turn eighteen. I'll be okay. I thank him and take the cold train ride home.

I hope something bad's happened to Aunt Janet. I won't forgive anything less.

– – –

"This is Janet. Can't come to the phone right now. Leave a message after the beep."

Beep. I hang up. Only so many messages a machine can hold. Lord knows it's full of mine.

She must be on the road, maybe with car trouble. I've been trying her for half a day. It's kept me busy, not thinking about other things. Like why G'ma never told me about my aunt in the first place. Only Janet knows for sure.

"This is Janet–"

– – –

I've got a bright dream of the old house in New Orleans. I've seen it in a picture, the place where Mama grew up. Mama's standing on the steps with G'ma's arm around her. She's younger than I am now. Another little girl in a yellow dress with skinned knees sits on the top step next to them. All three of them have got that same pretty smile. In my dreams I'm also there, sitting on the steps next to Aunt Janet. G'ma goes inside to make us lunch, and the three of us play jump rope games with all the songs Mama taught me when I was little, but I want to go inside with G'ma–

– – –

Bang bang.

Bang.

I wake up with a start. Someone is knocking at the door. I jump up from the couch, blanket twisted all around my legs. "I'm coming!"

My voice is cracked, sleepy. They don't hear me. The knocking stops. My throat goes tight. It might be Janet. I don't know what to say to her.

I yank open the door.

It's Mr. Mason, the maintenance man. Mason's big and

round in the face, with a body like a bull. I used to be scared of him, but he's a puppy dog.

"Hey, Miss Kendall. Didn't know you was in. Sleepin', huh?"

My hand goes to my hair. Nappy as a bush baby. Wrapped in a blanket and looking like I haven't bathed in the three days since G'ma's funeral, which is true.

"Yeah." I clear my throat. "Yeah."

"Sorry about Mrs. Wright. She was a good old lady."

"She was," I agree. "What's that?"

"Uh . . . it's a new lease." He hands me the fat envelope he's been fidgeting with and looks away.

"But we're year to year, I thought?"

"Your grandma's on the lease, not you. An adult's got to sign this thing. Someone gonna be your legal guardian now, or something? If they'll let you live on your own here, you can stay, but that paper's got to be legal."

I just stand there, staring at him. Legal guardian? Lease? "Mr. Mason, I just lost my grandmother. Can't you just let this . . . wait?"

He shakes his head. "Rent's going up all over the neighborhood. You got to sign a new lease before it hits here next." Mason shrugs, palms up like there's nothing he can do. I guess there isn't.

I drop my blanket, grab the letter with both hands like it'll make more sense that way. Mason won't look at me.

"I'm sorry, Miss Kendall. Them's the rules. You've got ten days to figure something out." His eyes are dark as chestnuts. "Different managers these days. Different rules."

I choke back tears with a laugh. "I guess everything's different now." Deep down inside, a small part of me had actually been thinking, worrying about getting back to school soon, finding some sort of job maybe, trying to get my life on track. What a joke. One letter from the management, and all the extra credit and after-school jobs in the world won't keep me living in the only home I've ever known.

Mason shifts from one foot to the other. "Don't you got somebody who can help you out? One of them can sign for you. That's legal, too."

A big hot tear drops onto the lease papers. And another before I realize they're mine.

"Yeah, I got family. Somewhere."

"There you go." Mason smiles like it's all settled, then. "Give 'em a call. Tell them what you need. Send it overnight if you have to. It'll be okay that way."

I imagine my letter going unanswered, like my calls. "Thanks, Mr. Mason. I'll handle it."

Ready or not, Janet, here I come.

6

I feel it before I see it. The air's been getting thicker for hours and the AC on the bus can't do a thing to stop it. We're down south now, and even in midwinter, the Louisiana weather is seeping in through the cracks.

"Newwww Orrrrrrlinnnns!" The bus driver sings the stop out as we come in down the freeway. The first thing I see is the Superdome sports stadium, a big half-domed building, like a cupcake that got squeezed in the middle. I recognize it from TV. The rest of downtown New Orleans is a blur around the Dome. It all disappears as we enter the bus station.

Off the bus, the air is thick with exhaust. I push my way inside to the ticket counter.

"Where can I get a cab?"

"Out front." The ticket counter lady points through a

pair of glass doors. I shoulder my bag and step outside to get my bearings. Canal was the place to be seen when G'ma was a girl. She would walk past all the department stores and fancy boutiques to catch a movie with her mother. From the way she talked, I could tell G'ma loved it.

Canal's nothing to look at now. Two streets running next to each other in opposite directions, with a streetcar track running along the strip of grass between them. They look like that cable car in the Rice-A-Roni commercial, two green cars hooked together, adding to the traffic on Canal.

The cab driver I get is an old man in a crushed hat, chewing on a toothpick. He looks at me in the rearview mirror when I get in, and nods.

"Twenty-seven eighteen Claiborne Street." I tell him the address from memory. The paper I wrote it on all but disintegrated on the bus ride down, I read it so many times.

The cabbie nods again and we pull into traffic.

Canal Street goes from skyscraper to two-story brick and stucco walk ups. Bars, car dealers, drugstores, little shops in buildings that look like the one I live in. Beauty parlors with hand-painted signs. Not the carnival Mama used to talk about when I was little. But every city has its neighborhoods, I guess.

As it turns out, Aunt Janet's is not the best part of town. "Careful out here, now," the cabby says to me, and drops me off across the street from what looks like a shorter version of the Chicago housing projects–bruise-colored brick apartments dropped elbow to elbow on a dead grass lawn. A couple of dim-eyed kids stare at me, and I cross to the far side of the street.

2718 Claiborne is what G'ma called a shotgun shack, a long, low house, one floor, with cement steps leading up to the two side-by-side doors. It's actually two houses in one, lined up like the barrels of a shotgun. Up north they call them railroad apartments, because you go from room to room the way you move between cars on a train.

Aunt Janet's shotgun shack might've been yellow once. Now it's just faded to an old-paper ivory color, with the wood showing through in spots. The shades are down, no lights on inside, but it's Saturday night. She might be out. I look up and down the street, trying to guess which car is hers. Then again, if she's out, that'd probably be gone too.

My hands feel hot and dry, but my neck is starting to sweat. Now my hair will get even frizzier and I'll look a mess when she opens the door. Just knock, get the signature, and get out. The bus back to Chicago leaves in four hours. This time Monday, I could take a shower in my own apartment again.

I climb the stairs before I lose my nerve and my hair gets any worse, and ring the doorbell. Nothing happens. After a minute, I knock. When no one comes, I ring the bell again. Screening phone calls is one thing, but hiding from the doorbell is just plain strange. This time, someone comes out of the apartment next door.

Dark as me and twice as wide, she's too old to be Aunt Janet. Aunt Janet was Mama's little sister–she'd be in her mid-thirties by now. The lady walking by me is fortysomething, at least. She's talking to someone inside the house.

"I'm sorry, Miss Clare, but I can't do tomorrow for free again. I gotta work, and work just don't come for free. I can't be giving my time away like that."

Another woman comes out. Miss Clare, I guess. A tired-looking white lady with fingers twitching like she's looking to hold a cigarette, but she's not.

“I’m sorry too, Alba.” She stands in the doorway, leaning against the screen door. It’s like I’m watching a play. Nobody even looks at me. Everybody’s got their own drama, I guess.

The older woman, Alba, stops at the bottom of the steps and turns around.

“I’ll come back when you can pay me, Miss Clare. I hate to leave you two in a bind, but you understand, I got my own bills to pay.”

Miss Clare shakes her head, red-blond hair falling out of its twisted bun. “I hear you,” she says. “I’ll give you a call.”

Alba leaves, walks off down the block the way I came, sneakers catching on the cracked sidewalk. The screen door slams and I come to my senses. Miss Clare is looking at me through the wires.

“Can I help you?”

I’ve got spiders crawling up my neck. “Huh . . . hi. My name is Kendall Washington. I’m looking for my aunt, Janet Wright. I think she lives next door.”

Miss Clare looks at me hard. “Oh, I know your aunt, all right,” she says in a way that makes me shift my feet.

“Don’t know what to tell you, honey. Your aunt Janet took off out of here like a hot streak a week ago without leaving this month’s rent. Left me high and dry trying to make my bills.” She looks at me again, at the bag on my shoulder. “But I’m guessing you didn’t know that.”

“No.” I drop my bag. My knees buckle, but I keep on my feet. Maybe she headed up to see me after all. “I came down from Chicago to see her. My grandma died. Her mother.” I look up at this stranger and smile a stupid, tired smile. “She’s my legal guardian. I just need her to sign a lease for me.”

I should've packed myself away with the rest of G'ma's things back in Chicago. My face wrinkles. I'm going to cry. Why didn't I just wait for her?

"Hey, hey, now." The lady steps outside. "What's your name, honey? Kendall, you said? I'm Clare. Clare Morreal. This is my house. I was renting the other half to Janet. Now, call it being Christian, but I can't leave you crying here on the front porch. Hold up a second. I've got the key next door. We'll go over. See if there's any clue when she'll be back."

I breathe real deep to smooth out my face. It works, for now. I straighten up, and pick up my bag again. Clare comes back with a key.

"Here you go." She unlocks my aunt's door.

There's a sad little sofa in the living room, with a dirty rug that leads into a dingy little kitchen. There's a phone on the living room floor by the sofa with an answering machine. I cross the room and press Play.

"Aunt Janet? Are you there? It's Kendall . . . Kendall Washington."

The sound of my voice is embarrassing. I try to shut off the tape, but it keeps playing. Message after message of me. "I missed you at the funeral. I hope everything's all right. . . ." I turn down the volume.

"Poor thing," Miss Clare says. At least she knows I'm not lying. "Maybe she called your cell phone?"

I shake my head. "I don't have one." G'ma was on a fixed income. It kind of stops you from moving into the modern age. Like I said, she wouldn't even listen to CDs.

"Hold on, maybe she finally made it to Chicago and tried to call me there." I fumble through my bag. "Can I make a call?"

Miss Clare shrugs. "It's your aunt's dime." I nod gratefully and find the sheet of paper with Mason's number on it.

"Mr. Mason? This is Kendall Washington. . . ."

"Hey, baby girl! How's your trip?" He sounds so far away and familiar. I miss him the way a sleepwalker misses his bed. I didn't know I'd care.

"I'm fine. Fine, thank you. Listen, I was supposed to meet my aunt down here, but maybe she went straight on to Chicago. Have you seen–?"

"Sorry, nobody been around here in a few days. Just Mrs. Alonso asking after you. You should send her a postcard."

I listen to him babble on, and my own head feels empty. "Yeah. I will," I tell him. No Aunt Janet. Where could she be?

"I got your note, and things'll keep here for a few more days, Miss Kendall."

"Thanks, Mason. I'll be back soon."

I hang up and sit there, kneeling on the floor, stuck in the moment of silence that follows.

"What'd he say?"

I start, and stand up. I'd forgotten Miss Clare was behind me.

"Uh, no luck. How long ago did you say she left?"

Miss Clare shrugs. "Sometime last week."

"Nineteen hours down, nineteen back," I calculate out loud. Maybe she called me up there, didn't get me, and turned around. "She could be back any day now."

"I certainly hope you're right," Miss Clare says.

There's a bed in her room, one of those big white and brass numbers. I open the closet. A couple of dresses are hanging there. "She'll be back," I say firmly, wrapping my hand around the metal frame of the bed. Miss Clare shakes her head.

"That old bed was here when she moved in. Too big to fit through the door." She rattles the bed with a hand. "My ex built it in the room. Now I just throw it in with the rent."

"Oh." There's nothing left to hunt through here, just bits of trash and the dresses in the closet. Old dresses, from the look of them.

"Well," I say, because I have to say something. It hangs there in the air, useless.

Bang bang bang. There's a knock on the wall.

"Aw, hell," Miss Clare mutters to herself. "Just a minute, Evie!" she calls out. I step back to let her by. "Excuse me. That's my daughter. I've gotta go."

"Wait," I blurt. "Sorry. I just–do you know where else I might find her?"

Miss Clare gives me a bittersweet smile. "Honey, if I knew that, at least I could sue her for the rent."

The banging comes again, louder. It sounds like it's coming from inside my head now.

"How about a hotel, at least?" The thought of hunting around a strange city at night is just plain dangerous. I can stay the night. Find her in the morning.

Miss Clare shakes her head. "Afraid not. Not one that's safe, anyway. Try up Canal a ways. Fancy, but clean."

"I can't afford clean." I look around the room. "Not that kind of clean, anyway." Think fast, Kendall. Think fast. "Can I stay the night here? It's still my aunt's place. . . ." I start to argue, then realize she hasn't paid the rent this month. I reach into my own pocket. "I'll pay."

Miss Clare blinks at me. "Well . . . the Lord helps those who help themselves, after all." She bites her bottom lip.

Next door, her daughter bangs on the wall again. That makes her decision. "Okay, forty bucks and you can stay the night. Things'll look different in the morning."

I dig the money out of my bag. Slim pickings, but I've got nowhere else to go.

Miss Clare gets red in the face when she takes it from me. "I wouldn't do this, but I've got things on my end too."

Bang bang bang!

"Hang on, Evie. I'm coming." Miss Clare shrugs at me, pockets the money, and leaves through a door in the wall I thought was a closet.

It turns out shotgun shacks are like Siamese twins, joined at the hip and the elbow, with doors in almost every room. Kind of like a hotel suite after all.

It's not even seven o'clock, but I'm beat. Nineteen hours on a bus can drain the life right out of you. I take a sweater out of my bag, use it as a blanket, and set the duffle on the bed as a pillow. I wish I had G'ma's records with me. The blues would go down well just about now. You'll find her in the morning, Kendall, I think. I shut my eyes tight until I fall asleep.

7

My stomach wakes up before I do. Last thing I ate was a pack of those bright orange cheese crackers pasted together with peanut butter. I sit up and hang my feet off the edge of the bed for a while, feeling sleep-stupid. My head clears a little and I remember. G'ma is gone. Aunt Janet's gone too. Lord. What do I do?

My stomach growls. Move, Kendall. Move or you'll never move again.

I force myself to my feet and check out Aunt Janet's fridge. There's one egg in the egg tray. Looks like it broke in there a long time ago, all cemented to the plastic with yellowish goo. I shut the fridge and grab my wallet. There's a liquor store or something on the corner, I think. At least I can get more orange crackers.

I hide my bag under the bed, and slip a piece of paper between the lock and door so it won't shut me out.

It's late morning and the neighborhood is full of noises, mostly little kids playing somewhere I can't see them, and car doors slamming, traffic from the next block over. Church bells announce the end of services as I head toward the traffic. Sure enough, I find what I'm looking for.

The corner store looks more like a house than a grocery store. A fading red sign says Lil' Sam's Food and Liquor. In Chicago, a place like this would be mostly liquor, with some candy bars for food. Here, it's like a supermarket shrunk down to keychain size. There's only one aisle of liquor, all its own at the far side of the store. I grab a carton of milk from the back, a loaf of bread, and some peanut butter, and pay at the checkout counter. The old man behind the register has watery brown eyes with whites the color of elephant ivory.

"Hey, baby girl," he says to me.

"Good morning." I turn my head. I haven't brushed my teeth, but the old man doesn't seem to notice.

"Afternoon, actually," he says. I stare. I must've slept longer than I thought.

"Haven't seen you around here before," the old man says, but it's not a question. I answer it anyway.

"My aunt lives about a block from here. Janet Wright."

The old man takes a hard look at me. I wonder if he's the Lil' Sam the store's named after, but he doesn't look so little in person. Suddenly, he smiles. Big bright teeth, dentures, like G'ma's, when she remembered to wear them.

"Aw, you're Miss Janet's niece? Haw. Didn't know she had family around here."

"She doesn't," I say, and it makes my voice catch in my

throat. "I'm down from Chicago. My grandmother passed away last week. I was hoping to find her. Janet, I mean."

His smile fades and he swipes his hat off his head like he knew G'ma personally. "Aw, that's a damned shame. A damned shame. I haven't seen your aunt in some days now, baby girl. But if she ain't home, most likely she's at work. Have you checked there?"

I feel so stupid. Stupid I didn't think of it. Stupid to hope.

"She does hair in a beauty parlor about three blocks from here. Take a left at the corner. Place called Maisy Dae's. Them women be up in there all hours talking and yakking about nothing. I bet you'll find her there, all right, for sure."

"Thank you, so much." I want to leave a tip, but you don't do that with cashiers, so I say thanks again.

"You take care of yourself, now." He winks at me.

Outside, I pause on the corner to get my bearings. There's a kid across the street looking at me. Tall and lean for a little kid, but not as tall as me, and skin like a chocolate chip. He doesn't smile, or wave. Just stares. I decide not to stare back.

The road ends a block past his head. Instead of road, there's a smooth green hill. Too high to look over from here, it looks like it goes on forever. Maisy Dae's is to my left. I go to find my aunt.

— — —

I can hear the place from a block away. Radio's blaring so loud, I'm surprised the street doesn't shake. Grass grows out of the sidewalk cracks like crazy hair right in front of the shop. The front window is half covered by the black outline of a lady in a pink hat painted on the glass, the brim tipped down over one eye with her manicured pink nails. The rest of the window is lined with posters of hairstyles and relaxer ads. Through the clear spots, though, you can see the women inside. Maisy Dae's looks like some kind of party.

Nobody turns around when I come in. There's a little bell on the door, but you can't hear the jingle above the music and the talking. The door shuts behind me and I wait, searching faces. Now I realize I don't even know what Aunt Janet really looks like anymore. She could be just about any one of the women here. Maybe she'll look like Mama or G'ma. But no one here fits the bill.

"Can I help you, hon?" a big woman in a blue smock asks, coming over. She gives me a second look, and her face wrinkles up. "Ooooo, girl, look at that featherbed mess of a head. We gonna get you straightened out in a minute. Just have a seat." She picks up a magazine and starts to walk away.

I fight the urge to smooth out my hair. It wouldn't do any good anyway.

"Actually, I was just looking for someone. Does Janet Wright work here?"

"Janet? Naw, I'm afraid not. She left out of here not more than a week ago. But don't worry, Nadine over there can help you out."

She points to another woman who's running a hot comb through a little girl's hair. "Nadine's our best at heat pressing, and real good with tender heads, just like Janet. She'll take care of you."

I feel numb. "I'm not here to get my hair done. I'm looking for my aunt. Janet Wright."

"What?" The magazine lady gives me a third look. "Yeah, yeah! You do look a little bit like Janet. Nadine," she calls across the room. "This girl here says she's Janet's niece."

"Hey," Nadine says, looking up from the hot comb in a way that scares me. I've burned myself more than once dragging those damn metal things through my hair. Then you've got to wear bangs to cover the scar, and as soon as it gets humid out, poof, there goes that slick hairdo. It's a wonder anyone presses their hair down here, damp as it is.

"Sorry, honey," the magazine lady says again, smiling and nodding her head. Then the smile disappears. "But we ain't seen your aunt in a week, like I said. Left us full with appointments we couldn't take. Downright dirty thing to do. Don't know where she ran off to either. If I did, I'd give her a piece of my mind."

I scramble to think of anything that can help me. If I leave here without a lead, I'm dead in the water.

"Maybe she has another job? Another beauty parlor, maybe?"

The magazine lady laughs. "I don't think so, honey. Janet had more work here than she could handle. Some man or other was always willing to pay for the rest."

"She had a boyfriend?"

The lady shakes her head. "Or three. There was always somebody. Never met them, though. Janet kept all that stuff at home."

And home is a dead end too. All I can do is sigh. "Well, if she comes back here, could you let her know I'm at her place, looking for her?"

"Sure thing," the magazine lady says, and walks away. I look around the beauty parlor one more time. It smells like burning hair and lye. But there's nothing to tell me what happened to Janet.

"That girl ran off with some man, I bet," I hear Nadine whisper to her customer.

"Mmm hmm," the magazine lady agrees, and uses the magazine in her hand to sweep some hair off the counter. "Always said she was no account. No account, indeed."

I want to go back and ask them what else they know about my aunt, but if they can't tell me where she is, then I guess there's no point. Outside, the air is cool and a thousand times better than in the beauty parlor. I take a deep breath and slowly walk the seven blocks back to Aunt Janet's old address.

Clare's daughter is sitting on the front steps when I get there. What's her name? Evie.

She could be anywhere from fourteen to my age, the way her small body sits draped inside a black wheelchair. Thick glasses and straight brown hair, the kind I would kill for, and pale skin that makes me think it's not such a good idea to sit out in the sun like that. Still, I don't say anything. I've got no small talk in me.

Apparently, she does.

"No luck?"

"Nope." I take the wedged piece of paper from the door frame and hold open the door.

Evie looks at me sideways. "Didn't think you would."

"Why not?" I've come a long way to find Janet. Why should it be this hard?

"Some people just don't want to be found, is all."

"And why would my aunt be one of those people?"

She shrugs, awkwardly because of the wheelchair.

"And you know so much about her."

"Not her," Evie says. "About them. People who disappear."

I wedge the paper back into the frame. I haven't talked to anyone in days it seems, really talked. I sit down on the stoop next to her chair.

"Like Houdini?" I ask.

"No. Just people. Like your aunt."

"My family's not like that." I sound so sure of myself, I realize I believe it. "Way I was raised, family sticks with family, and that's that."

"Yeah." She shrugs again. A lot, I realize. Like it's a nervous twitch. "It's only been five days. Maybe you're right."

"I know I'm right. Besides, I just need her to sign some paperwork, then I can get out of here."

"What kind of papers?" Evie looks at me through those big glasses, and suddenly I don't want to be out here explaining my life to some kid. I want to find Janet, and I want to go home.

I get up, bones stiff with standing around and worrying, and wiggle the paper stopper out of the door. "Is your mom in?"

"She's taking a nap."

I rummage through my pocket and come up with another two twenties. "Do me a favor and ask her to let me stay another day."

Evie nods at her fingers. They twitch a little, like a current's running through them all the time. "You can give it to her later. I'd just drop it."

"Okay." I pocket the rent money. "Thanks."

"Why don't you just forge it?"

"What?"

This girl's staring at me, a little smile hiding in the corner of her mouth. "Her signature. Why'd you come all the way down here when you can forge it?"

"Why–" Good point, Evie. Good point. "Because," I say. Just because.

I shut the door behind me.

Why not just forge the damn thing, Kendall? Why spend the last of your money looking for somebody you've never even met? I should be back home, looking for a job, convincing my teachers to give me another chance at school. But the truth is, I'd be here even without the lease to sign. I'd be here because G'ma asked for forgiveness, and only Janet knows why.

There's no TV in the apartment. No food but the peanut butter, bread, and milk I bought this morning. Not even a sofa. I make myself a sandwich, take out the carton of milk, and go sit on the bed. I should've bought a magazine. A magazine would be nice, or coffee. That's what cops do on stakeouts. That, and look for clues.

And that's when I think of what that girl said. Aunt Janet's been gone for five days. G'ma's funeral was six days ago. She left too late for the funeral. She wasn't going to Chicago at all.

I put away the milk and walk the apartment, front to back. My stomach is boiling with acid anger. Where *is* she? What could G'ma possibly have done to make Janet lie to me and run away?

I swat through the clothes on their hangers. I kick the mattress on the bed. And end up back at the answering machine. It's one of those old tape things, not a digital machine like most folks have now. I sit on the living room floor, flip the tape, and press Play.

"Janet, baby." A man's voice. I lean in to listen. "Baby, call me." Beep.

“Janet, where you at?” The same voice. “Call me.” Beep.

“Hi, Janet, this is Carl.” Another man.

“Hey, Carl–” It’s Janet’s voice now. My aunt. “Let me shut this off.” The machine clicks. The rest is left to my imagination.

The women in the beauty parlor said she had boyfriends. Carl must be one of them. The acid in my stomach settles. You’ve got a lead, Kendall.

I flip the tape back around and sit there, hugging my knees. I should’ve bought a magazine.

I close my eyes. Eight months of late nights keep catching up with me, I guess. I drag myself to bed and fall asleep.

8

Somebody's crying. Kumbaya. Wake up, Kendall. Somebody's crying. G'ma's crying for you again.

I'm out of bed before I can think about it, racing down the hall toward her room, but the door's not where it should be. I'm in a hallway that doesn't end. Maybe it's a dream. But I've got to get to G'ma.

I pound along the wall, following the sound. It's coming from the other side of the door. I yank it open, run in, run to the bed, kneel down. So dark I can't see my hands in front of my face, but her hand is where it should be. I grab it.

"It's okay, G'ma. Shush, shush. I'm here." G'ma grabs hold of my hand, tight. Too tight. She's getting stiff on me. "G'ma?"

My eyes are getting better. It's not G'ma. It's that girl. Clare's daughter, Evie. I'm in New Orleans. G'ma's dead.

Evie squeezes my hand, but she's not seeing me. Her eyes are rolled back so only the whites are showing, lids fluttering like sheets snapping on a line. She's rigid and I realize she's having a seizure.

"It's okay," I say again, but I'm scared. I think back to health class, to G'ma's first stroke, and there's nothing to do but sit it out and try to keep her calm.

"Why should I be discouraged. . . ," I say hesitantly. "When trust I have in Thee? His eye is on the sparrow, and I know He watches me." My voice never gets stronger, or louder, just steady enough to keep the tune. I don't know if it helps the girl, but it helps me. I kneel next to her, my hand crushed inside hers, and eventually the seizure passes.

Evie's eyes focus on me all of a sudden, and her muscles go limp. She sits up, gasping like she's been underwater. I pat her back, then stop myself. She's not choking. She looks scared, like she's had a nightmare, or something worse.

"I'm okay, I'm okay." She waves me away. I back off and see the rest of the room. The living room is the mirror image of the one next door, except instead of being empty, there's a sofa and a television. Evie's propped up on the sofa, made up like a bed with blankets, white sheets, and a pillow. Behind the sofa, against the side window, is a tiny table covered with mail.

I look back at Evie. Even with my bad night vision, she looks pale.

"Could you turn on a light?" she asks.

I stare around stupidly.

"There, on the wall by the door you came in."

I find the switch. We blink at each other in the new light.

"I didn't mean to bust in on you like that," I tell her, hovering by the doorway. "I didn't know it was still unlocked."

"S'okay." Evie puts a hand to her head like a woman in a migraine medicine commercial. "I'm glad, I guess. Seizures scare me."

"Epilepsy?" I ask.

"No, better," she smiles. "Muscular dystrophy. They throw the seizures in with the wheelchair and the bum legs."

"Lucky you."

Evie looks around the room. So do I. "Where's your mom?"

"Hmm? Oh, she got a late call from the hospital. Usually she doesn't leave me alone. When she finds out about this, she'll freak. She's worse than a watchdog."

I think about me running home to see G'ma at lunchtime and nod. "Who used to stay with you? My aunt?"

Evie snorts, and it's not pretty. I get the feeling my aunt is not very well liked by anybody except the men on her answering machine.

"Yeah, right," Evie says by way of confirmation. "Your aunt was hardly ever here, and if she was, she had company and wasn't checking in on anyone."

I cringe. "You make her sound loose."

"Do I? Sorry. It was always the same guy. Until the end. But he was . . . I didn't like him. The first or the last one either."

"Was one of them named Carl?"

Evie shrugs. "We weren't exactly introduced."

"Right." Another dead end. I make a mental note to ask Lil' Sam, the grocery man, in the morning.

"Do you know where I can find either of them?"

She shakes her head. "Most of the time they just picked her up and drove off. I used to try to guess where they were going, but I couldn't tell you for sure."

Evie yawns, stretching her arms over her head.

"Well, I'm up for a while now, I guess. Want some hot chocolate?"

I think about my dinner of peanut butter and milk. Hunting down Carl can wait. "Sure."

Evie grins. "Mind making it? I'm a disaster in the kitchen."

"You haven't seen me," I warn her.

"You're bluffing."

I shrug. "Yeah."

With Evie's directions, I find the cocoa powder and milk, and a suitable pan to get things going. Blame it on the time of night, but maybe Evie's not so bad.

"What was Chicago like?" Evie lolls her head back to watch me from the sofa.

"Cold."

"It's cold down here."

I look at her. It's got to be almost sixty degrees outside. The day I left home, there was a high of four. "Not like Chicago," I reply. She concedes with a shrug.

"And? What else?"

"I don't know. Never really thought about it." I cut the milk off before it gets all filmy, and add the cocoa. "It was just home."

Evie doesn't say anything, which is fine by me. It feels like something's swelling up inside my throat. I'm allergic to thinking too much. "I miss my grandmother."

"Cups are in the second cupboard." Evie gestures with her chin. "Your grandmother, she raised you?"

The question makes me laugh. I'd gotten so used to taking care of her in the last few months, I'd forgotten it was the other way around. "Yeah, since I was five. Rest of my family died in a car accident. For some reason, I walked away. People used to say I was special because of it. That God was watching me. But maybe I just got thrown away." I shrug. "Say, can you drink this straight?"

"Add a shot of bourbon," Evie smirks. "And a straw, maybe. They're in a box on the countertop."

I get one of the bendy straws for her and sit on the edge of the sofa, her mug in one hand, mine in the other. "Couldn't find the bourbon."

Evie leans forward enough to sip through the straw. "S'all right. I'm cutting back." She holds out an unsteady hand. "Gives me the shakes."

She takes a sip of cocoa through the straw. "Hey, the straw's not melting."

"Ice cubes," I explain with a smile. Evie looks at me accusingly.

"You've done this before."

"When G'ma finished taking care of me, I took care of her. She had a stroke last summer, took her strength. Couldn't get around much without me." I blink and the tears stay away. "But we did okay."

"I don't get it," Evie declares. "I mean, I look at my mom. One day she doesn't have a care in the world, and the next there's me and she's chained down for the rest of her life, or mine. Whichever. Even I'd resent me. Didn't you hate it?"

I realize I'm staring at Evie. "Hate it?" I sound dumb, but I repeat it anyway. "Why? Wasn't much I could do about it, either way. Besides, family sticks with family. That's the cardinal rule. And G'ma was all I had. How could I hate it?"

Evie studies my face for a moment, then shrugs. "My dad did." She takes a sip of cocoa. When she speaks, her eyes stay on the cup. "When I said people disappear, he was one of them. He and my mom split up when I was a baby. So last year, when I turned sixteen, I tried to look him up and I found him. Married. A normal kid named Jake or something like that, and a wife that works at Winn-Dixie . . . that's a grocery store. He'd forgotten all about me. Didn't even know my name. When I told him who my mother was, he hung up on me. Just like that."

Evie's eyes are on the edge of her cocoa mug, but they're seeing something from a long time ago. "Didn't even remember my name. And you know what? My dad didn't leave my mom until I was a year old. A whole year, and it didn't matter. Just forgotten about, like that." She snaps her fingers so loud, I almost drop her cocoa. I wouldn't have thought she could even make contact with her thumb.

"That's not right," I say inadequately.

Evie snorts. "Hey, I only lost a dad. Mom more than makes up for it in sheer effort. She blames herself for everything, for my father leaving, for my MS. Like if she'd been living right, been with the right guy and all, I'd have been perfect. But she wasn't and so . . ." She waves a hand at her useless legs. "My mom actually thinks a couple of cigarettes and some over-the-counter medicine when she was pregnant did this to me. She'll do anything I ask to try to make up for it."

There's a mischievous glint in Evie's eye that worries me. "You don't use your mother like that." I don't want to believe it. G'ma would've strung me up if she caught me taking advantage of anyone, especially her.

"Why not?" Evie asks. "She thinks she owes me. It makes her happy."

"Family doesn't take care of you because they 'owe' you," I explain. "They do it out of love."

"Like your grandma took care of you?"

"Yes."

"And like you took care of her. Not because she raised you, but because you loved her."

Suddenly, I don't want the hot chocolate. I put both cups on the floor. "What do you mean?"

Evie sighs. "I'm just saying that guilt and obligation are thicker than love."

The hot chocolate tastes like ashes in my throat. "If that's the case, G'ma took care of me because she felt guilty about my parents' deaths."

"Probably." Evie nods.

"And I took care of G'ma because I owed her for taking care of me."

"Stands to reason." Evie nods again.

I shake my head. I almost let this girl get to me. But she's wrong. "And where does your dad stand in this picture? And my aunt?"

"Guilt is thicker than love, but fear is thicker than guilt. I think my dad was scared of the responsibility of having me around. Just like your aunt."

I stand up, take the half-finished cocoa cups to the sink. I don't want to think about my aunt right now. "I've had enough pop psychology for one night. You're too young to be so miserable."

Evie smirks. "I'm older than I look."

"Even so." I wash the cups, set them to dry and head for the adjoining door.

"Thanks for the hot chocolate. I'm going to bed."

Evie's mouth twists in disappointment. "Hey, Kendall? Why'd you come over here tonight?"

"Because you were crying."

"So."

My hand feels hot on the cold doorknob. "And because I thought you were my grandmother. I thought she needed me."

"Wouldn't you call that guilt?"

"No."

Evie presses her lips together. "Do you want a job?"

I give a confused laugh. "What?"

"You heard me."

"All I want to do is find my aunt."

"Right, so she can sign your papers and you can get back to Chicago." She waves her hand. "But what about the meantime."

I've got school to worry about, and social workers, the rent . . . I don't have time for a "meantime." I want to find Janet and go.

"What about the meantime?" I ask.

She gestures the way G'ma did, encompassing her entire disability in one flick of the wrist. "Well, obviously, I could use some help around here. It's not as tough as it sounds. Tonight was the worst of it, if you ask me. I'm just here most days. My high school isn't exactly accessible, so I take my classes online." She indicates the desktop computer against the wall. The kind of setup I'd have killed for back home. Things might have been different if I could have taken classes from home. My thoughts drift to G'ma, but Evie's talking to me. And if wishes were horses . . . I turn back to the girl in front of me.

"I still have to go in for proctored tests," she says. "Like the PSATs. All you'd have to do is take me to the school down the street tomorrow. Put ice cubes in the cocoa, tell me when I'm full of crap. The last lady, Alba, hardly did much more than that."

I'm so tired, my head feels like Jell-O. I shake it and it wobbles on its stem. "I'm going to bed–"

"Think about it." Evie reminds me of an evil mastermind, sitting on her sofa, propped up by pillows, hands folded in her lap. They twitch every so often with unspent energy.

"Good night," I say.

"Good night."

– – –

I get up in the morning and have to think about it a bit before I get into the shower. I don't know why I'm still here. Janet's disappeared. The bus back to Chicago leaves in the afternoon. I should be on it. But not without a bath first.

It's strange, being in somebody else's house, like Goldilocks just waiting to get caught. The bathroom's in need of a good scrubbing. No towels left behind, nothing in the medicine cabinet either. I'm about to look under the sink when I realize that with every move I make, I'm searching for clues about Janet. But she's not the only reason I'm still here. I can't face the apartment without G'ma in it. Not yet. Or going back to school, a week too late with my extra credit and a whole week behind again. It feels like high school slipped through my fingers in the handful of days between G'ma's death and Mason's new lease agreement. Maybe I'm just hiding out down here in New Orleans. Maybe I'm not ready to face the real world.

I shake my head and cut off the water. Nothing's simple. Not today.

I stand on my sweater when I get out of the tub to dry off, and I get dressed in the same square foot of space. I feel achy on the inside, like my bones want to rest somewhere easy. But easy's gone out the window now. I leave my bag inside the doorway and go outside to see what I can see.

It's early, sun's just up. Looks like I finally caught up on my sleep again. The air is as thick and humid as ever, but it's getting to be fall, so there's a coolness to it. This is a little side street. No buses run down it, but I know from my cab ride that a walk two blocks to the corner will take me to a busier street. I want to see the French Quarter today. Ride a trolley car up St. Charles Avenue. Yeah, Chicago can wait one more day.

"Had breakfast yet?" Evie's screen door bangs open as she wheels herself halfway onto the porch. She's dressed already too, with a blanket over her legs. If I didn't have to go to school, I'd never see this side of seven a.m. There's something about this girl I can't get to the bottom of.

"Nope," I reply.

"You hungry?"

"Sure."

"C'mon, then. Biscuits are in the oven."

Inside, Clare runs around, trying to get curlers out of

her hair and breakfast on the table. I help by mixing the orange juice, the frozen kind in a tube. The biscuits are hot, and sweet with butter and honey.

"You like grits?" Clare asks.

"No, ma'am. My grandma liked grits. I think they're nasty, no offense."

"None taken." Clare smiles. "I used to think so too, but they grow on you. Especially with eggs and a little ham."

"And butter. G'ma took hers with butter."

"Yep, gravy, too," Evie suggests.

I wince. "That's nasty."

Evie and Clare laugh at me. It's an easy sound, one I used to make with G'ma. It's nice to hear it again.

"So, Kendall, Evie tells me you've had no luck finding Janet. What are you going to do now?" Clare is staring at her coffee cup now, not me.

"I have to get back to Chicago. I've got things to take care of."

"I wish there was something more I could say." Clare's got something else she wants to tell me, but doesn't. I look at Evie, who gives me an innocent smile. I know what she's thinking–forget it. I look away.

"Kendall, listen. Evie told me about her seizure last night. I just about died knowing I wasn't here. But you were. You took real good care of her too."

She looks up at me and I see deep-set worry in her eyes. "Evie's my blessing, but I can't be here twenty-four hours a day. I know she's a handful, but I need help.

"Evie and I . . . we . . . we were thinking we could help each other out. If you're willing, maybe you could stay on as a caregiver, just for a few days, in exchange for rent. You'd be able to stay here, look for your aunt, and it would give me time to find a replacement for Alba. Evie's getting to the end of her homeschooling. Does it all on the computer now." Clare points to the workstation crammed between the TV and stereo. "Real convenient for a working mom. And today, she's got her PSATs in an hour, down at the elementary school. I can't take her. I've begged too many sick days off work. Evie keeps telling me she can take a cab, but . . ." She hesitates. "We could make it, you know, room and board? Three meals a day."

"I–" I can't think of what to say. Forty dollars for two nights isn't much to pay. Maybe I owe them something. And the PSATs . . . G'ma took me down to take mine. I stare at the biscuit in my hand, brown and sweet with honey in the middle. I can't take my eyes off it. Maybe I don't have to go back. Mason said I had ten days. Today leaves me with eight.

"You get *Mary Tyler Moore* down here?"

"Heh," Clare chuckles. "You like that show?"

"I watch it."

"Yeah," Clare says, "I think it comes on, late at night, though."

"I can do late nights."

Clare puts down her coffee cup and looks at me. "Let's see how it goes, then."

I nod, and smile. "Let's see how it goes."

This whole time, Evie's just been sitting there, quiet as a chair, letting us talk. I give her a look. She returns it with a little smile that makes me shake my head.

"Satisfied?" Clare asks her.

Evie shakes her head. "Don't dawdle, woman, I've got a test to take."

Clare gets up from the table, shaking her head. "This

girl's gonna be the end of me. Shoot, and I'm gonna be late for work."

I stand up too and start clearing the table. "I can't get you to work, but I think I can handle your daughter."

Evie pushes back her wheelchair and laughs. "Try me."

Something tells me I've just made a devil's bargain. But it doesn't matter. I've got eight days to figure out the rest of my life.

9

It's hot today. Sitting in the sun doesn't help. All the elementary schools in New Orleans are named after the same man, John McDonald, so you can't just say you go to McDonald Elementary. It's got to be McDonald #6. I wheeled Evie up #6's front door ramp to a room on the first floor, made sure she was set up in front of a computer like the one she has at home, with a mouse in easy reach, and a modified keyboard she can type her answers on. I had no advice for her. School for me seems so long ago, I can't remember how to take the kind of tests you write down. Only the ones life throws at you, and I'm not doing so good at those, either. Instead, I wished her good luck. But Evie looked so relaxed, I doubt she needed it.

Sitting outside McDonald Elementary School #6, waiting

for Evie to finish her PSATs, I can't help but think luck's something I could use.

"How come you come to N'awlins?" It takes me a minute to realize someone else is asking the question, even though it's running through my head.

There's a skinny kid standing in front of me who wants to know the answer too.

"What?" I say. I should've just ignored him, but it's too late.

"You don't go to school here," he says, like that explains his question.

"No, I don't." Part of me still wants to ignore him, but it's been a long wait. Company is company. "I saw you outside Lil' Sam's the other day."

The kid nods. "So how come you don't go to high school or something? You too old for school?" He's got a basketball under his arm, and gangly dark brown limbs, torn jeans, a brightly striped rugby shirt. Hair shaved so close you can see the shape of his head. He can't be more than ten or eleven.

"No, guess not. I just don't go."

"Yeah," the kid says, and sits down next to me. He bounces the ball.

"You live with that cripple girl?"

I close my eyes and remind myself he's just a kid. "She's not a 'cripple.' And no. I live next door."

"S'cool," he says. "I seen her once or twice in her backyard. Mom's Miss Clare, right? Real nice lady. Real nice."

"She seems to be," I say.

"So, how come you sitting out here instead of in school?"

"I'm taking time off." As I say it, I realize it's true. I'm taking time off from life without G'ma. Remembering she's gone makes me tired. I turn to the kid and change the subject. "What about you?"

"About me what?" He puts a foot up on the wall I'm sitting on.

I glance at my watch. "Shouldn't you be in school too?"

The kid shrugs. "I'm out sick today."

I raise an eyebrow. "You don't look sick."

He kicks the wall beside me with a sneakered toe. "Yeah, well, I'm sick of school. So I'm staying home."

I shrug. "Suit yourself." I can't exactly lecture him about the joys of staying in school.

"You ever been to Alabama?" the kid asks. He bounces the basketball once. The random question startles me.

"No."

"Yeah." He nods like he expected the answer. "You don't sound like you're from Alabama. N'awlins, neither." He looks at me with sharp brown eyes. "Where you from?"

"Chicago."

"Chicago." He repeats the word like it's a new flavor, then nods, smiling. "I got family in Chicago. My daddy's cousins on his daddy's side."

"Wow. Big family." I shift a bit on my seat. This wall's starting to feel hard, and I think the kid's a little on the weird side.

"How come you come to N'awlins? To take care of Miss Clare's girl?"

"No."

"Then why?"

Nosy little boy. I want to shake him by the collar. "Why do you want to know?"

The kid shrugs and looks away. His arms dangle, resting

on his knee. "Just trying to make conversation. You know, be polite."

Suddenly, I sound like G'ma, all huffed up and annoyed at his question. "Polite would be telling me your name."

The boy gives me a level look. G'ma might've been able to rattle him, but not me. "Marcus," he says.

"Marcus, I'm Kendall." I shake his hand reluctantly. Hurry up, Evie. I want to go home.

"Pleased to meet you," Marcus says, and I can tell its something his mother taught him to say. That makes me smile.

"Likewise."

He kicks the wall a couple more times and we both watch the dust rise from his shoe. "Is it true you're looking for your aunt?"

There's no point in denying it. I nod.

"She was a pretty lady. But I never knew her much."

My heart skips a beat and I sit up a little straighter. "But you knew her some?"

"Yeah," the kid says proudly. "I know everybody some bit. I even knew who you were."

I stand up at attention. "What do you know about my aunt?"

"She seemed nice, like I said. Smelled like lilacs. Had a lot of boyfriends, but my mama said she wasn't no hooker. Just a pretty lady with lots of men around. And a mean one named Chuck or something. Once I went up to look at his car, just look at it, and he yelled at me. Wasn't even that nice a car. But it had fuzzy dice and I'd never seen that before, for real."

I drop my head between my knees. *Wasn't no hooker.*

"That's good to know," I say. He's talking bad about my aunt, and I can't even get mad at him. I mean, if G'ma stopped talking to her, she could be the Wicked Witch of the West, for all I know.

"What's so good about a mean boyfriend?" Marcus asks. I look up at him to see if he's joking. He's not.

I shake my head. "No, that's not what I meant. But wait. You said this guy's name was Chuck? Could it have been Carl?"

Marcus shrugs. "I dunno. Whatever his name was, he wasn't somebody I wanted to know."

I sigh. Another dead end. Janet's disappeared off the face of the earth. All I can do is hope she gets back by the end of the week, because come Saturday, the ten days will be up on Mason's eviction notice. Either way, I've got to leave.

Sorry, G'ma, I think to myself. You can't get forgiveness from someone you can't even find. I wish I could have seen her, just to know what she's like.

"Marcus, you don't know where she is, do you?"

Marcus shakes his head. His basketball's on the ground now. He rolls it around with his foot. "Naw. She just left one night. I remember 'cause my cousin saw them trying to move that bed out. He said they couldn't get it through the door."

The words hit me in the face like ice water. She tried to take the bed. *To take the bed.* I sit back down on the wall again, breath gone, head pounding with a sudden rush of adrenaline and blood. Aunt Janet's not on the road to Chicago. And she's not away for the weekend. She's gone for good, and she's not coming back.

"What'sa matter?" Marcus asks.

"That bed was built in that room," I tell him, and I feel far away from my own voice.

Marcus doesn't notice. He just nods. "That's what my cousin tried to tell them."

"Them?"

"Yeah, her and that mean guy, Carl or Chuck or whatever."

Yeah. Whatever. A sigh rises up out of me before I can stop it. The sigh should've been a scream. I put my head in my hands. Marcus's basketball bounces up against my leg. I don't want to cry in front of him, but I don't know how to get him to leave. Instead, I kick the ball back to him. He kicks it back at me, and we pass it for a couple of minutes.

"I got a soccer ball back at home. It's better than this for kicking."

I look at Marcus and I feel so screwed up inside, I'm going to cry anyway. I want to be back home in Chicago on the sofa watching TV, with G'ma down the hall bugging me for a glass of water. I want to be asleep in first-period chemistry, with the other kids passing their homework in over my head. I want to be anywhere but here, with this skinny little kid telling me my jerk of an aunt ran away when I needed her most, tried to steal a bed when she left, but she's no hooker, no siree. Not at all. Not a hooker. Just a liar and a tramp.

I swallow hard to keep my tears down. "Sorry," I say. "I've got to stay and wait for Evie." I'm amazed at how even my voice sounds. I clear my throat. "Rain check?"

Marcus gives me another hard look but doesn't pry. I pick up his ball. Marcus takes it. "What's a rain check?"

Maybe he's younger than eleven after all, and just tall

for his age. I relax my shoulders. "It means maybe another time."

Marcus grins. It makes me want to smile a little too, but I can't. He reminds me of my baby brother, Mackie.

God, I don't want to be alone.

"See you later," he says, and heads down the sidewalk, bouncing his basketball as he goes.

"Who was that?" Evie calls to me from the doorway of the school. I must have missed the bell. The test proctor waves from the doorway and goes back inside. Kids are opening up the windows as the day grows hotter.

I stand up and shake off my blues long enough to respond. "Hey, Evie. How was it?" I jog up the stairs and help her wheel her way down the ramp.

"Fine, I guess. Tests are tests." She blinks her eyes at the sun.

"Yeah." I hunker down and we roll back to her house in silence.

10

"I've got something for you."

Inside the house, Evie makes her way over to the CD rack. I sit on the sofa with a glass of iced tea, numb. Feels like my heart is one big string and God's just plucked at it so it won't stop humming. I hurt. But I've got to keep it together at least until Clare comes home and I can be alone.

The CD comes on without the soft hiss a record player makes. No wonder G'ma didn't like those things. The music sneaks up on you before you know it, and suddenly, someone's singing over your shoulder, right into your ear. It can scare you silly.

But not this song.

It's Sarah Vaughan, singing something sweet and low over the speakers. One of G'ma's lonely-day songs. It sounds like a smoky jazz club on a warm summer night.

Like I'm being wrapped up inside one of G'ma's old blankets. I sit on the sofa with my iced tea and start to cry.

Evie doesn't hear me, and I'm glad she can't. She's lost in the music, wheeling back and forth in her chair, humming along. I lean on the side of the sofa, rest my head on my arm, and let it all out. Silent, shoulder-shaking sobs. First G'ma, now Janet. How many more people can leave me alone?

Mama, Daddy, Mackie, too. Everyone.

The worst part is thinking I never really knew my grandmother, not if she could keep a secret like Janet from me. It's like when she died, the truth of who she is died too. When I can't cry anymore, I look up slowly. Sarah Vaughan's on to song number three, and Evie's staring at me.

I wipe my eyes. "My G'ma used to play that song when I was at school. I called it her lonely-day music. It makes me think of her." It's only part of the truth of what's going on. But it is all I want to share with this unpredictable girl.

She looks at me a moment longer. I look away. I don't want to be here anymore. I don't want to stay the rest of the week. I don't want to stay the night. I want to get on the road again. I still got a life to figure out back in Chicago, on my own.

"Evie, I've gotta get out of here."

"Then get your coat," she says. I do a double take. Not what I was expecting. But she's not saying what I think. She points with her chin. "I want to show you the river."

Oh. I can feel a low headache coming on. I close my eyes. I could use some air.

"Let's go."

– – –

We step out into the cooling afternoon. The sky is still blue but going kind of purple. The streetlamps are starting to light up. It's beautiful and soothing, after being in the sun all day.

"Which way?"

Evie points down the street, to where the road ends a few blocks away. That hill I noticed the day before, green and soft in the afternoon light, runs perpendicular to the end of the road. "What is that?" I ask.

Evie smiles. "The levee. And the Mississippi."

The levee is like a big dam, or one of those dykes in Holland, a man-made hill built to hold back the river. We pass Lil' Sam's on the way and someone calls out from the shadows under the store awning.

"Hey."

I look around. It's that boy from this morning. Marcus. He's staring at Evie in her wheelchair. "Hey, Marcus." I tip my chin at him and he falls in behind us.

"You know him?" Evie asks curiously.

"Marcus," I say, "this is Evie. We met outside the school today."

Evie nods at him warily. "You're Mr. Broussard's grandson, from the store?"

Marcus breaks into a grin. "My reputation precedes me," he says proudly, like he's imitating someone he knows. My heart feels like a lead weight, but Marcus looks so genuinely happy to be recognized, I smile too. Evie does not.

"Come on, Kendall," she says. I forge ahead.

Marcus skips to catch up. "Hey, where you goin'?"

"To the levee," I tell him.

"All right, then," he says gruffly, and kicks the ground

with a scuffed high-top sneaker. I squat down a little to get a grip on the sidewalk and heave Evie's chair forward.

We get to the bottom of the levee and I can see train tracks running along the bottom of the hill. Evie and I wheel up the road and cross the tracks.

"There's a park on the other side," Evie says. From where I'm standing, that little hill looks to be straight up. Evie's chair rolls easy, but not that easy.

"Okay." I take a deep breath. "Hold on tight." Evie's fingers flex in the air. Looks like she's revving a motorcycle. I step back a ways and take a running start. "One, two, three!" I crouch down and push my arms against the back of her wheelchair, dig my legs in, and start running up the hill.

"C'mon, c'mon, c'mon, c'mon!" I keep pushing. Evie's laughing at me, and I'm losing my breath, trying not to laugh too. Halfway there. My legs are getting tired. Almost there. My legs are jelly. "C'mon," I say, but I don't feel it.

And then someone's pushing right along with me and I look up and it's Marcus, pushing Evie's chair over my head. "C'mon!" he yells at me when I stop pushing to look up at him. We hover on the hillside for a second. Then I throw myself back into the push and it's easy as pie; one two three, we are up and over the top of the hill.

"Now," Marcus says with finality.

"Wait!" Evie calls out. We've stopped, but her chair hasn't. I race to drag her to a stop before she goes all the way down the other side.

Marcus catches up to us with long, easy strides. "Cool chair," he says to Evie.

"Thanks," Evie says dryly.

"And thanks for your help," I add. Something's eating at Evie. I'll save it for later. I push Evie up a ramp onto the little sidewalk and take a look at where we've gotten to.

We're standing in a little park on a pathway through the grass. A bathroom and a little gazebo are up ahead, near a couple of picnic tables. And then there's the water, the mighty Mississippi. It looks like a wide black highway with no painted lines in the twilight. Up where the river bends, I can see lights twinkling on big old barges floating down the water like eighteen-wheeler trucks.

"What do you think?" Evie asks me.

I catch my breath. "Look at that." We've got the river in Chicago, and Lake Michigan, but nothing this big could fit on the Chicago River and still go under all those drawbridges.

I wheel Evie over to one of the picnic tables, set the brakes on her chair and let her face the river. I step up onto the bench and sit on the tabletop next to her. The early evening cools around us quietly.

"You don't like me much, do you?" Marcus asks Evie.

All I can do is blink. Evie looks him dead in the face. "I don't know you."

"But you could," he says.

"Evie–" I start to interrupt, but she doesn't let me. Evie's face hardens.

"You had your chance, too. I've passed you and every kid on the block a million times. None of you've ever said hello before."

Marcus looks at his feet. "I wanted to. But some days you just looked so dang mad."

Evie gets a look on her face–shock, anger, frustration,

all at once. "What do you expect? I'm not deaf. I can hear it when people are laughing at me."

Marcus scowls. "Shoot, we weren't laughing at you. We were laughing at Alba. She'd be all out of breath from pushing you along. It looked funny." He shrugs.

Evie makes an exasperated sound that reminds me of Charlie Brown missing the football. Only, Marcus is the one who's missing the point this time.

"Laughing at someone is still laughing at someone," I say.

Marcus waves my superior morals away. "Aw, you guys don't know Alba. She told my mama she ran the Sugar Bowl marathon last year. All uppity about it too. But you've seen her. She can't walk a mile. That's why we're laughing."

I look down at Evie. Slowly, a wry smile creeps across her face. "Alba's not even pushing me. I usually have to wheel myself."

"You see?" Marcus says, justified. Even if it's wrong, I laugh.

Evie takes a deep breath, and I can see the rest of her anger slipping away. She plucks at the arm of her wheelchair. "I'm not that bad, you know," she says. "Not really."

Marcus accepts it with a nod, and slaps the back of the wheelchair. "I gotta go to the store for my mom," Marcus says. "But I'll be back in twenty minutes. In case you need help getting back over the hill."

"Thanks, Marcus," I say. Evie manages a half smile and keeps watching the river as Marcus runs off, all legs and elbows, over the levee.

"What was that all about, Evie?" I ask when he's gone. She waves a hand in the air.

"I don't like to be made fun of."

"Yeah."

"Yeah."

Evie and I sit in silence for a while. The air smells green, like rain's coming, the air cooling to a crisp edge. It's beautiful. Peaceful. I just sit there and breathe.

The first stars are coming out by the time Marcus comes back and helps us over the levee as promised. We stroll back slowly. Clare's pulling up to the house down the street.

"See you around," Marcus says when we reach the grocery store. "I live down there." He points to a bunch of sad brick row houses across the street. It doesn't take me long to recognize the look–these are the projects.

"See you, Marcus." Just for a minute, I feel something tickle in my throat. I miss having friends. Even if they're just little kids. It makes me wish I could stay here longer.

Marcus tugs at his ear nervously, like he wants to say more, and changes his mind.

"Bye, Evie." He waves at us and lopes off toward home.

"Bye," Evie says softly. She's looking at us. At me. I raise an eyebrow and she looks away, frowning.

"What's wrong?"

She shakes her head. "You're leaving, aren't you?"

11

We stop there in the middle of the sidewalk, staring at each other. Evie doesn't blink. I can't lie and I don't look away.

"Yeah. Marcus told me what I needed to know this afternoon. My aunt's not coming back."

"You promised to stay the week," Evie says, arms crossed. I start to push again. I've paid to stay here. I don't owe them anything.

"I said we'd see how it went, and that's how it's going. I'm not going to find her. I'll tell your mother tonight."

Evie shakes her head and folds in on herself. We roll back to the house in silence.

— — —

"Hey, girls." Evie's mom smiles at us from the kitchen. "I just got home myself. Settle in and we'll see about dinner."

"Help me to the sofa," Evie says. She doesn't look at

me. All business. I bend down to help her move from her chair to the couch and she grips my neck real hard.

"Hey, Mom, did you know Kendall was thinking of leaving?" Evie calls out so loud, I almost drop her.

"What?" I gasp.

"What's that, honey?" Miss Clare calls from the kitchen. The water is running, lucky for me. This isn't the way I want her to find out.

"Nothing," I call. I fix Evie with a hard look, the one G'ma used to give me to get to the bottom of things. Evie looks back at me, her eyes sad, but there's a hard little smirk playing on her lips.

"But you are, aren't you? I was just a meal ticket for a couple of days. Your aunt didn't show, so you're out of here."

I set Evie firmly on the couch and straighten out her legs and look her in the eye. "Look, I told you and your mother when we made this agreement that I had other obligations." I shrug, and shake my head. "Besides, what difference does it make to you? You barely even know me."

She's silent for so long, I have to look up to read her face. Evie's smirk turns into a cold smile. "Oh, it's not me it matters to. It's my mom. I already get the big picture. People. Leave."

I stand up slowly until my head is twice as high as hers, and step back from the couch. Not the way I wanted this to go, but I've got my own problems. "I guess they do."

Evie looks away from me. "Poor little Marcus. He thought he'd made a friend. But you don't have friends, do you?"

My throat, my voice, gets tight. A kid I've known one day can put a lump in my throat, just because he reminds me of my little brother. It surprises me. I take it out on Evie. "Why are you so mean? Do you think you're the only one in the world with feelings?" I get in her face. "Girl, you don't know me. You don't know what I'm about."

"Sure I do. You're like your aunt. You're loy-al." She says the word slowly, in two parts, and makes it sound shameful. I want to shake her. I want to pick up her wheelchair and throw it across the room. Janet has nothing to do with who I am. Nothing at all.

"Yes, I am," I agree angrily. "But not to you."

Miss Clare comes into the room just as I slam the door behind me.

"Evie, what did you say?" I hear her voice through the door. If Evie answers at all, it's too quiet for me to hear.

I want to scream, but they'll hear me. I want to rip this house apart. Instead I pace up and down the long rooms, pounding the hallway, until I realize they can hear that, too. Then I sit down on the bed, my face in a pillow so they can't hear me cry.

In all the days I took care of G'ma, all the times she kept me up at night, scolded me, drove me nuts, I never hated her. But I hate her now. My mother, father and brother, too. I hate them all for leaving me. Maybe Aunt Janet's just doing what comes naturally to my family. Nobody but nobody sticks around.

If Aunt Janet walked through that door right now, I'd kill her for leaving, for doing this to me.

"But she doesn't even know you."

The voice in my head is G'ma talking good sense. But she's gone.

It's only then that I realize I've said it myself.

— — —

Night closes around both sides of the house and I see the light go off beneath the door to Miss Clare's living room. Her footsteps sound heavy. She must be carrying Evie to bed. I lie on my back in the bed that was too big for Aunt Janet to steal, staring at a water stain on the ceiling, like a dark ring bleeding through the pale paint. My stomach feels like curdled milk inside me. Stupid Evie. And I let her get to me.

I roll onto my side and stare at the wall. I don't want to go back to Chicago. I don't want to be in that apartment all alone, even if it's only long enough to pack and leave. But there's nowhere else for me to go.

Lying here in the dark isn't helping. I can feel every muscle in my body telling me to do something. But what?

After a second, I climb out of bed and pad my way into the front room, lit by the streetlight falling through cracks between the curtains. The telephone and directory are where I left them, in the middle of the floor. I drop to the floor cross-legged, and dial my own number.

"We can't come to the phone right now, leave a message." Beep. I hesitate. It's weird to hear my own voice over the line. And that stupid message, too. G'ma didn't want me saying our names because people might guess we were two women living alone and rob us in our sleep. At least, that was her logic. In the end, we stuck to the basics, just a hint more personal than the robotic voice the machine defaulted to after a power outage.

Before the tape can run out, I dial in the code to check messages remotely.

"You have three new messages," the robot voice says.

My heart thumps against my rib cage. I press the pound

key, and the machine announces the first message, left the same day I arrived in New Orleans.

"Hey, Miss Kendall, it's Mason, your building super. I just wanted to see how you was getting along. Awful sorry about Mrs. Wright, again. If you need anything, just give a call." He leaves his number. I save the message and press pound again.

I close my eyes. A woman speaks.

"This message is for Kendall Washington. My name is Anne Bigford, I'm the social worker assigned to your case. First, let me say I'm sorry for your loss. I understand from Ms. Tabara, the social worker at Grant Memorial, that your aunt is assuming guardianship. Please call me as soon as possible so we can walk through the paperwork together."

I stifle a laugh. Only a few days ago, I had such great ideas about Janet and me, how we were going to be a family. It's amazing how things can go from bad to downright awful in next to no time. I play back the message and write down the number. There's a new knot in my stomach. I don't know what happens to kids without guardians. Oliver Twist and David Copperfield don't make it sound so great. I crumple up the number. It can't come to that.

Beep.

"Good afternoon, Miss Washington. My name is Mary Johnston. I'm with the funeral home. We just wanted to do a follow-up call to see if you were pleased with the service we provided. We hope you'll call on us again. Gravenstein Brothers is glad to be of service in your time of need. God bless."

I almost choke on my laughter. "Call on you again?" I hang up the phone without saving the third message.

"That's just crazy," I say to myself. Why would I need Gravenstein's now? Everybody's already dead.

The words bounce in my head and my stomach drops. I crawl to the window and open the blinds until there is enough light to read the phone book. When the hearse came, they took G'ma to the county morgue for a death certificate and then to Gravenstein Mortuary. My fingers shuffle through the pages until I find the county morgue.

"County," a woman's dry voice says over the line.

"Huh . . . Hello. I'm looking for my aunt. . . . Ja-Janet Wright." I swallow hard. "Do you have someone under that name?"

"This is the morgue, honey, not the hospital. You'll have to call another number for that."

My hands are cold, but my face has gone hot. I stay on the phone by force of will. "No. I know it's the morgue. My . . . my aunt is missing, and I wanted to check . . ."

I run out of words.

"Missing?"

Silence crackles across the line.

"Hold on, dear." I hear fingers on a keyboard. "I swear, administration is always messing this up. They should have notified your family if the body was being taken to the morgue."

"Oh," I say softly, and wait. Aunt Janet should've notified me herself, I think. I close my eyes. Please say she's not there. Please.

The woman sighs. "I'm sorry, honey. Nobody by that name here. You might check with your aunt's hospital. Sometimes they keep them overnight."

"Right. Thanks." I take a deep breath. "Are there any other morgues in New Orleans?"

"They all come through us, eventually. All right? Bye, now."

I hang up the receiver and lie back on the worn rug. Janet Wright. At least she's not dead. Then again, I might be better off if *I* was.

I laugh, but it turns into a sigh.

I stay there on the floor for a long, long time.

There's a knock at the front door. It's early, but I'm already up and dressed. I'm leaving today. I'm so tired, so achy from lying on that hard floor that I don't care if it is Aunt Janet or the Abominable Snowman, they can wait. Yeah, right. I end up running the last few steps to the door.

It's Clare. She's dressed for work and looks worried. My face tightens and my heart falls. "Thought you were my aunt."

"Sorry, Kendall. I know it's early. I just . . . I figured out what happened last night." Clare's fingers twitch like she's holding a cigarette. She looks tired. "Evie . . . Evie can be a handful sometimes. I told you that. But don't let it get to you."

I have a hard time holding that tired gaze. "Miss Clare, I was just here to find my aunt. I've got to get home to Chicago. That's all."

Miss Clare's eyes grow even wearier. "Aw, Kendall, I understand, it's just . . ." She drops down onto the front step. She looks funny sitting there in her nursing uniform. After a moment, I join her. "Look, Kendall, I have to go to work, I can't leave Evie alone. And I'm not finding anybody else to take care of her.

"Evie's a handful, like I said. And the closer she gets to finishing high school, the worse it is." She looks up at me with a half-horrified little smile. "You know what she said? She wants to go to college. College. She's never even left the house by herself. Tell you the truth, when you came along I thought, we'll see. With all of her homeschooling, Evie's never really been around other kids before. And she seems to like you."

I have to laugh at that one. "Don't know where you got that idea."

Miss Clare gives me a serious look. "I know it's bad, but that's how she shows affection. Used to hurt me something awful, like she's picking fights just to be mean. But it hasn't been easy on her, all cooped up in here all day. And the schools that could have taken her are all just too expensive, or too far away. Even then, we'd still need day care when she got home–I don't know. I've done this wrong, maybe. But I'm trying. Lord knows I am."

She falls silent for a moment, and I feel so uncomfortable, my skin starts to itch. "I wish I could help you, but–"

Miss Clare jumps in before I can finish. "You can. Just one more time. Please. Watch her for me today. I'll have something else figured out by the time I get home."

I shake my head. "I was going to the bus station today. My aunt's not here, I'm not going to find her. And, quite frankly, I can't be around your daughter."

Miss Clare keeps her eyes locked on me. She's desperate and it makes me nervous. "Please. There'll be another bus tomorrow. She should be fine alone in a room. Just . . . just check in on her once in a while. If there's a problem, call Tulane Hospital. They'll page me."

"Miss Clare, I–" I what? Don't like your daughter or the way she makes me feel? It sounds too petty, even for me.

"Kendall, I didn't need to take you in. Please. Return the favor."

And that does it. Guilt buttons being pushed left and right. Evie was partially right about why we do the things we do. I take a deep breath and clasp my hands together. "Okay. I'll check on her." Chicago can wait one more day. And so can Ms. Bigford, and Mason and the apartment.

"Great." Clare sighs, relieved. "You don't even have to make her lunch. I left some sandwiches. It'll be fine. And thank you. Thanks." She backs off the steps and hustles down the walkway to her car. Halfway there, she turns around.

"She really does like you, you know." She smiles.

I just shake my head and watch her get into her car. When she's gone, I head back inside. Time to make your own plans, Kendall. Make your own plans.

The way I see it, I can get a job to pay for G'ma's apartment, or I can go to school and starve. Information gives me the number to my high school. I don't recognize the voice of the front office lady who answers. Good. Leaving a message seems easier than facing Mrs. Robinson, after all the leeway she tried to give me. But I should at least let them know.

"Hi. Um . . . this is Kendall Washington. I'm a senior. I won't be finishing the rest of the semester. Could you let my teachers know?"

The office lady tells me it's a shame, and pulls my file. "Oh, Kendall Washington. We were sorry to hear about your grandmother."

"Thank you." It feels weird, still fresh, hearing those words in a Chicago accent.

"We'll need a letter from your guardian before we can excuse you from class."

"Um . . . okay." I close my eyes. If I can forge a lease, I guess I can forge a letter, too. Whatever it takes.

"Now, Kendall, we hope you won't give up on school entirely," she's saying.

"I wish I didn't have to. But I've got to find a job now."

"Let me see," the woman says. I wish I could see her face, know who was on the other end of the phone. "You were almost done with classes, Kendall. Would you consider going for your equivalency degree?"

"What?" I'm caught off guard. "Like I've said, I'm calling to drop out, not start up again."

"Oh, no," the woman says. "I meant get your GED. It's a test you take, for the equivalent of a high school degree. That way, you can go to college when you're able. I hate to pry, but your grades are mostly good, and you're so close. The test will be harder, the longer you wait."

Test. The GED. I can finish high school after all. G'ma would be proud. I would be proud.

"How do I sign up?"

"They offer the test every few weeks. I think the next one is next week or so. Should I put your name down?"

"Uh . . . yes."

"They'll send registration materials to your house."

"No. No, can you send them to a different address instead? I'm at my aunt's right now."

The woman takes down the New Orleans information. I write the test date on the flip side of the lease envelope. Friday, March 3rd. Nine days from now. It'll be like graduating three months early.

"Study hard, now, and you'll do fine."

"Oh . . . okay. Thank you. Goodbye." I hang up, stunned.

I can still finish school. Little shivers of excitement dance up my arms. They speed up my spine and turn into a case of the nerves. Study hard, she says.

One thing about me–I don't do well with tests. I can know the stuff backward and forward, but when you sit me down with a pencil and a Scantron sheet, it's like my mind goes completely blank. Hysterical blindness, G'ma used to call it, but she said "hysterical mindlessness" instead. Generally, it was my overall grades, not my exams that made me a decent student.

My heart skips a beat in my chest. I can feel my lungs start to wheeze. My palms sweat, and my head grows hot. Hysteria. A minute ago, all I needed was a job and a legal guardian. Now I need a miracle.

I sigh huge. My shoulders feel tight. How am I going to do this?

First things first. My fingers feel numb, but I pull out Mason's lease and Janet's old letter. Her name is on it in simple cursive. I practice it a few times on the envelope the lease came in, and sign the paperwork on the dotted line. Sorry, G'ma, but nobody else was going to do it for me.

Then I hear the music. Sarah Vaughan comes floating through the wall, sweet and sad, like the end of summer. *Pennies in a stream . . . falling leaves, a sycamore . . . moonlight in Vermont.* From Evie's, right next door. And she's just taken the PSATs, no sweat. Against my better judgment, I need to talk to her.

I open the middle door. The lights are off, sun filtering through the shades, it's like being in a brown and pink cave. "Hey."

The singing stops, but the music keeps on playing. Evie's alone. Guess it wasn't Sarah Vaughan singing after all.

Evie looks up from her pile of CDs, frowning. Her eyes brighten ever so slightly when I walk in, then take on that old tough look. But it doesn't work. She's been crying. She puts the CDs on top of the stereo.

"Hey."

I shut the door behind me and do a quick study of my feet. She tries to look uninterested, and fails.

"Should I say I'm sorry?" she asks, surprising me.

"Should I?"

She looks at me a long moment, and I can see something struggling in her face–pride and loneliness. I recognize them both. She shakes her head slightly and makes my question easier to ask.

"Evie, I want to go for my GED. Will you help me study for it?"

Evie frowns at me. "Will you stay and help me?"

We stare at each other, blinking in the warm, dim afternoon light. The air smells like breakfast biscuits and menthol cigarettes. Clare must've been smoking again. I sit down on the sofa in front of Evie, our eyes on each other the whole time.

I fold my hands.

"Yes."

She considers, then nods. "Okay."

12

"But just until the test," I add.

Evie shakes her head, that old wry smile back on her face. "What's that?"

She nods toward the lease in my hand. I hadn't realized I was still holding it.

"Oh. I took your advice." I show her the lease. "It's due at the end of the week."

Evie smiles slowly. "I've got a stamp and I know where the mailbox is."

I smile back. "Hey, can I use your computer to write a letter to my school?"

"Sure."

Fifteen minutes later, signing Janet's name is starting to feel natural. Evie hands me an envelope. Is this the same girl who ripped into me yesterday like I was the worst traitor in the world?

"Thanks again," I say. "I'll be back soon."

"No, *we'll* be back soon," she says. "I'm coming with you."

If I hesitate at all, it's only for a second. It's better to be with someone than completely alone, even if that someone is Evie Morreal. We leave a note for Miss Clare, just in case, and roll out the back door.

Turns out the nearest mailbox is on the corner near Maisy Dae's Beauty Parlor. The place sounds the same as it did that first day–radio blaring, and women shouting back and forth at one another. It seems like another world from the one that Evie and I are in, on the cracked sidewalk outside. Evie sees me check out the shop through the window.

"Want to go in?" she asks me.

For some reason, I don't. It just seems like too much of a celebration in there. And maybe I don't want to hear any more comments about my featherbed hair, or see the sympathetic looks I got last time.

"No." I drop my letters into the mailbox. Goodbye lease, goodbye dropout letter. Godspeed. "That's it."

"Hey, hey," a woman says from behind us. "Ain't you that girl been looking for Janet Wright?" She's tall, with unshaven legs and brightly painted toenails peeking out of her flip-flops. By the size and intricacy of her hair, it's clear she's the latest creation of Maisy Dae's Beauty Parlor.

She comes up behind us, sucking her teeth. I nod. "Yes. My name is Kendall."

"You her niece or something, huh? The ladies told me about you last week." She nods back toward the beauty parlor.

Evie and I stay silent. The woman doesn't seem to be waiting for an answer.

"Yeah, well, I seen her. I seen her just about a week ago. At the Cabbage Rose, that bar up on Napoleon. They play blues some nights, and she's there for that."

I stand there stunned. "Uh . . . thanks. Thank you very much."

The woman breaks into a dazzling smile. "Sure, honey. Be good, now." She flip-flops off down the street, swinging her legs in the air like she's trying to dry her toenails faster.

"The Cabbage Rose." I repeat the words like I can taste them.

"What are we waiting for?" Evie asks.

"You know where it is?"

"No, but a cabdriver would."

I do a mental count of my cash. "How much is a cab?" Before Evie can answer, I shake my head. Even if it's my last cent, if it gets me to my aunt, it's worth it. "Never mind. Lead the way."

We wheel toward a bigger street and flag down the first cab we see. Evie's chair goes into the back, and we're off.

"Looking for someone is kind of like fishing," Evie says. "You drop a bunch of lines in the water, and wait to see if anything bites."

I see what she means, but I have to ask, "And exactly when was the last time you went fishing?"

Evie smiles wryly. "That would be when I went looking for my dad. I did Internet searches and made phone calls. It took forever."

"But it worked."

Evie shrugs. "Yeah, it worked. But it didn't work out. Not the way I had planned, anyway . . ." She looks at her hands. What if I do find Aunt Janet and it doesn't "work out" the way I planned either?

I shake myself to get rid of the bad feeling. Evie seems to realize the implication of what she's said, and forces a light laugh. "But, hey, I found him, at least. That's a start."

"Yeah, it's a start."

We pull up across the street from the bar. "You sure you girls want the Cabbage Rose?" our driver asks. He's only taken us six or seven blocks from the beauty parlor, but the neighborhood is night and day from ours. The houses look like the paint's been sandblasted off in spots, and the few houses with porches are sagging. A group of kids about Marcus' age stare at us from down the block, but they don't look like they want to make friends.

Evie and I share a look. The Cabbage Rose looks more like the cabbage part of its name. For a minute, I think it's just another house, but there's a little barbershop next to it, and a tiny dry cleaners on the other side, all sharing one low building that used to be painted white. The bar has a plate glass window, but the glare from the sun makes it impossible to see through.

"Well?" The driver turns in his seat to look at us. The sun goes behind a cloud, and the glare disappears from the front window. There are people inside. The chance that one of them is Janet is slim, but I pull out my money and pay the man.

"This is great, thanks."

He nods, pops the trunk and helps me haul Evie's chair out onto the sidewalk. "Thanks," I say again, and the cab pulls away.

Evie and I stare after it.

"Ready?" Evie finally breaks the silence. I take a deep breath.

"Yeah."

I wheel her across the street and maneuver the chair over the curb. The front door to the bar is open, with the screen door shut to keep the flies out. If the Cabbage Rose looked sketchy from across the street, being up close hasn't improved it any.

"Nice place your aunt picked out," Evie says, eyeing the shadowy customers through the screen door. Music drifts out, along with the smell of stale booze, sweet and sour, like fruit left in the sun too long.

"I take it you don't want to come in?"

She shrugs. "I'll be fine right here. Call if you need me."

"Right." I smile back lamely and push open the door.

The Cabbage Rose is not as scary on the inside as I thought it would be. There's a sticky wooden floor, a few black formica tables with those red faceted tulip-shaped candleholders you see in Italian restaurants sometimes, and a long bar facing the front window. It's warm inside, even though it's cool on the street. A ceiling fan works overtime, trying to make the place bearable. There are a few people at the bar, all men. No sign of Aunt Janet. I feel a little twinge of disappointment, and a surprising sense of relief. I guess the Cabbage Rose doesn't fit my idea as the ideal site for a family reunion. After all, it's only three o'clock in the afternoon and there are people at the bar.

"Can I get you something?" the bartender asks.

"Um. Maybe. I'm looking for someone." I hesitate, and then walk up to the bar. The place is so small that everyone will hear what I have to say, but maybe that's a good thing. It'll save time.

"Um, I'm trying to find my aunt, Janet Wright? I was told she comes in here sometimes. Do you know where she is?"

The bartender, an old guy with a face as round and

dimpled as a little boy's, wipes his face with his bar rag. "Janet Wright. Yeah, she's in here sometimes. Why you looking for her?"

I get a flutter in my stomach. "My grandmother, her mother, passed away last week. I came down from Chicago to tell her about it. She wasn't answering her phone. . . ." I trail off. This sounds pathetic. The bartender is staring at me, like he's waiting for a better story. I open my mouth to say something else, and a guy at the end of the bar stops me.

"Janet ain't here, sugar. She ain't been here for days now. But I know where she is."

I look down the bar at my informant. He's tall, all arms and legs, perched like a spider on his bar stool, with a beer glass in front of him. His shirt is unbuttoned over a worn-out tank top and stained khaki pants. In spite of his clothes, his face is handsome, with a neatly trimmed mustache and hair shaved to within a half inch of his scalp.

The bartender nods at me, or shrugs, I can't tell. I swallow my discomfort and make my way down the bar. "What's your name, sweet thing?" Spider Legs asks.

I take the bar stool he offers me. The little flip-flop my stomach is doing says not to tell him my real name, but if I don't, it'll make finding Janet that much harder. "Kendall," I say. "Pleased to meet you."

"Aw, shoot, she's got manners, too!" Spider Legs exclaims, and claps me on the shoulder with a bony hand. "Yeah, you could be Janet's niece after all."

I feel a little glow. It's the first good thing I've heard about Janet since I got here. She's got good manners too.

A second later, I realize that's not what he means. His eyes are checking me out in a way that shows no manners at all. I fold my arms and fight the urge to stand up and walk away.

"So, you know where she is?" I sound harsher than I mean to, but I can't help it. I lose the fight and stand up, stepping back from the bar.

"Hold on, now, hold on." The man takes a sip of his drink. "Now, Janet's a special person. Real special. Ain't that right?" he asks everyone at the bar. No one else is paying him any attention.

I take a gamble. "Is your name Carl, by any chance?"

"Carl?" Spider Legs practically spits the name out. "Carl? Hell, no, I ain't Carl." He stretches out the word "hell" so it sounds like a train speeding into the distance. "That's what I had to tell you. Janet don't come to the old Cabbage Rose no more 'cause she's with Carl now. Got herself a new man." He drags the last word out into a sarcastic drawl. "She with him, wherever the hell *he* is." Spider Legs hangs his shoulders over his head, his face low to his beer, then looks at me like he's seeing Janet instead, and isn't too happy about it. "Now that"–he jabs the top of the bar with a skinny finger–"is all I've got to say." With a *hrumph,* he turns his back on me and continues to nurse his beer.

I take a breath and regret it. The smell of Spider Legs' beer and the old ashtrays chokes my lungs. Nobody else says anything. I clear my throat.

"Does Carl have a last name?"

Spider Legs snorts and doesn't even look at me. I glance at the bartender, who just shrugs. "Most folks ain't got last names here, honey."

Right. I push away from the bar. My one lead, turned to so much cigarette ash.

"Thanks," I say to anyone still listening, and back my way out the door.

"Well?" Evie is hanging so far off the edge of her wheelchair, I almost hit her in the face with the screen door on my way outside.

"Any luck?"

"I wouldn't call it luck," I say. "She's gone, Evie. Just gone. No one knows where."

"Says who?" She sounds as incredulous as I feel.

I shrug, and wheel her away from the door. "Some guy. An ex-boyfriend or something."

"Really." Evie manages to make the word sound judgmental. "And you believe him?"

"What else am I supposed to believe, Evie? She's not here, she's not in Chicago. If she's in Venezuela or Katmandu, it all means the same thing."

We stop in the middle of the block. At least, I stop, and I'm the one doing the pushing. My hands are shaking. My head is shaking. My whole body is doing a dance of denial.

"G'ma wanted to see my aunt before she died." I shake my head. "Janet didn't have to be there for me, Evie. But she should've been for G'ma. She should've been.

"What am I going to do?" I rub my face with my hands. I feel so alone.

But I'm not alone. I'm with Evie, who says, "You're gonna take me home, and study for your GED."

The last thing I want to do is study for anything. I can't keep riding this roller coaster. I drop my hands from my eyes. "Do you know what my grandmother used to say about family?"

"What?"

"She said it was like cream, it stays together and rises to the top. You know what else she said?"

Evie looks at me expectantly.

"She said, 'Nothing but nothing sours like family.' "

Evie laughs, but not because it's funny. I start to push her chair again.

"When she said it, I thought she was always talking about other people. Not about us."

Now I wonder what soured our family, why G'ma cut her only living daughter out of our lives. Wish I knew. Maybe knowing would've gotten me that much closer to finding Janet. Then again, maybe knowing would be worse than never finding her.

Evie asks a question, but I don't really hear it. Instead, I hear a roaring in my ears, and a realization ripples across my arms like static, giving me goose bumps. My stomach clenches inside me.

"I think I'm going to be sick."

"Kendall? Are you okay?"

Evie's talking, but I can't answer her. I drop to my knees on the broken sidewalk, hang my head over the gutter, and vomit. Nothing comes up but water and yesterday's peanut butter and jelly.

I sit there, clutching the edge of the sidewalk, until the heaving subsides. The pebbles of the sidewalk dig into my hand. My head pounds with every heartbeat. God. What a mess.

"Sorry. That's gross. I don't know what happened."

I sit back up and feel better, but only below the neck. My head hurts, and just thinking about being sick makes me feel sick again.

I wipe my mouth with the back of my hand before I face Evie again. If the blood hadn't already rushed to my head, I'd be red with embarrassment. As it is, I can tell by her expression how bad I look.

Evie looks like she's seen a ghost. Pale as a glass of milk, her eyes staring right through me.

"Evie?"

For an instant, I see it, the fear of a small girl in a wheelchair a quarter mile from home, with the only person who knows who she is and why she's here collapsed on the side of the road. I thought I knew need before, felt it every time I stretched the umbilical cord between G'ma and me. But now, I can feel it full force, the snap and twang of it as I crumble to the ground and abandon Evie to the empty street, just as surely as Janet has abandoned me.

Then the moment is gone. Evie reaches for my hand. It's warm and clammy, but it anchors me back to reality. A pebbled concrete sidewalk, the tiny bits of rock chewed up and embedded in sandy cement. The worn rubber treads of Evie's wheelchair. Her withered legs, long as my own, but thin, like arms.

"Are you gonna be okay?" Evie asks. She's back to being whatever it is that makes her the girl I met on the steps two days ago. A girl with an edge.

I stand up slowly, and nod. "Yeah. I just . . . I just felt bad," I say lamely.

Evie accepts my answer, but she keeps shooting me looks the rest of the walk home, and doesn't bring up the GED again. We roll home, and I let the cool breeze mop the sweat from my face. I feel like I've had the flu. Like I could lie down and sleep for days. My stomach muscles ache from clenching, and my legs feel weak.

G'ma was right.

Nothing but nothing sours like family.

13

When we get home, I go straight to my room and lie down. Little beads of sweat keep clustering up on my forehead and above my lips. I wipe them away with my sleeve. The door between the two sides of the house opens with a cracking noise, and Evie rolls in. I barely turn my head to look at her. Something white fills her hands. It's a towel. A second later, she puts it over my forehead and eyes. It's wet. Cold. She doesn't make a sound. Just sits next to me for a minute, and then rolls away. The door stays open, just a crack.

I close my eyes and die.

— — —

Through the bus windows, the sky looks wet and gray. This must be Cairo, Illinois. Farm country. The grass looks too green to be true under all this rain. But it's not rain, it's sweat, isn't it? And there's a river running through the fields, wide and flat, with nothing but tall grass for a shore. I press my forehead against the window. It feels cool and flat on my skin.

A white station wagon with fake wood siding passes the bus. It's a Country Squire. The wagon keeps going and my eye is drawn back to the river. The sun lights up the water like liquid fire. Then I see it's not the sun. There's a person, standing at the edge of the river, knee-deep in blue-brown water, her white skirts tied around her knees.

She looks familiar. My heart sticks in my throat. Mama. No, not Mama. *G'ma.* Young, as young as Mama was when she died. Washing dresses in the river. Her hair is still dark and shining, curls held back with a red kerchief tied in back. She's so far away, but I can hear her, hear her singing.

Look at me, I'm as helpless as a kitten up a tree.

I sit up straight and start shouting to the bus driver to let me off. The bus keeps on going.

It keeps going, but I'm off it somehow, standing in the wind where the rain has died, there on the edge of the river. "G'ma!" I call. She looks up at me, a handful of dress in her right hand, basket held to her hip with her left. She squints at me, and the true sun flares up through the clouds, catching us both in its light. G'ma smiles.

"Virginia," she says. "Virginia."

— — —

I wake up with a start. My stomach is hollow, and my pillow is soaked in sweat, but my forehead is cool again. I feel better. I feel fine.

Still, it's a long time before I swing my feet off the bed. My cheek pressed into the pillow, my hip sinking into the weak mattress, I unfocus my eyes and try to see her standing there again. My grandmother. My mother. I miss them.

"Kendall." I say my name to bring me back to myself. "Kendall Washington. You've got to get up."

There's this thing G'ma used to tell me about. A spark, she called it, the Holy Spirit. She said it was the thing that keeps us going when all we want to do is lie down and die. It's different for everybody. For some folks, it's religion, belief in their God. For G'ma, it was family, someone to need who needed her, too. That thing that on the worst days of your life makes you get out of bed in the morning and carry on.

G'ma was my spark, my piece of the Holy Spirit, for the longest time. And then I tried to make her need for Janet *my* need. But that's like trying to light a fireplace full of wet wood. It just won't take.

"Kendall." I say it again.

Janet's nobody's Holy Spirit. Not the man in the bar, not the women at the salon. Not a single person I've met thought of Janet as good. And here I was, trying to use her to light my fire.

I see that station wagon pass me by in my dream, with a family inside. And G'ma, washing dresses. Girls' dresses, women's dresses. Baptism and wedding gowns.

"Kendall Louise Washington, this is your life." The line makes me laugh, even though I'm the one saying it. Like that old TV show G'ma used to talk about, where they surprise you with people you used to know.

I close my eyes, but my empty stomach won't be ignored.

"Get up," I tell myself. And I get up.

— — —

Evie's sitting at her computer, fingers flying so fast, she doesn't hear me come in. I clear my throat. "Hey."

She jumps, and tabs over to another screen so I can't see what she's been working on.

"Hey, Kendall." She doesn't sound the least bit guilty, but she doesn't look me in the eye for a minute. She rolls away from her computer desk and faces me.

"How do you feel?"

I shrug and sit down on the slumping sofa. "All right, I guess. Sorry about that."

Evie shakes her head and rolls over to her CD player. "Don't be. Everybody gets sick, right?" She stops shuffling through her music collection long enough to shrug and grin. "Heck, even me."

I smile too. "I can't remember the last time someone put a towel on my forehead," I confess. "Probably when I had chicken pox, when I was nine."

Evie puts a CD in. I don't recognize the music, and there are no words, just a clarinet leading the melody. She puts the jewel case back and looks at me. "And I can't remember the last time someone came bursting through that door to hold my hand when I had a seizure."

We hold each other's gaze for a moment. Then I blink.

"Are you hungry, or is it just me?" I hated Evie yesterday. And now I think she might be just about my only friend. I stand up too quickly and try to cover my confusion. "I've got peanut butter next door."

"My mom left sandwiches," Evie says.

"Shall we?" I head for the kitchen.

Evie follows me. "Let's."

When Miss Clare comes home at eight, Evie and I are sitting at the table looking over one of her old GED practice tests. Clare stands in the doorway, a bag of groceries in one arm. “Hey, girls.” She scans the situation, and relaxes. “Good.”

She puts the groceries in the kitchen and drops her purse on the table.

“Good.”

14

Over dinner, we tell Miss Clare about our plan–I play caregiver until the test, in exchange for a week and a half of room, board, and Evie's help studying. She agrees, says she's glad for the help. But I think she's even happier I'll be spending time with Evie.

"You'll need schoolbooks, won't you?" she asks.

"A prep book is a good idea," Evie agrees.

Three plates of smothered pork chops and rice later, we load Evie into the car and head into the French Quarter for a trip to the late-night bookstore, and dessert at Café du Monde.

"Ever had a beignet?" Miss Clare asks. She pronounces it "ben-yay."

"Nope. G'ma used to talk about them, though. Are they like doughnuts, or fried dough?"

Evie smiles. "You'll see soon enough."

My first time driving more than a few blocks in the city, and it's mysterious at night. The air is downright chilly and damp, like a cold, wet towel thrown across your face. I shiver even with the car windows up.

Canal Street at night is like a casino strip. The storefronts are lit up, and there are tons of people crowding the sidewalks, waiting for buses or going nowhere. Without meaning to, I find myself scanning their faces, looking for one that looks like mine. Clusters of tourists drift into the cracks between buildings that serve as streets in the old part of town. We take a wider route, following them along the river hidden just over the levee, and into the French Quarter.

"You're lucky," Clare says. "One more day, and this place will be packed to the gills with tourists and locals alike."

It looks pretty packed to me already, so I ask. "What for?"

Clare and Evie smile and answer me at the same time. "Mardi Gras."

Mardi Gras. I roll the word around in my head. Fat Tuesday. Now that is something I would love to see.

The bookstore is on the river side of the street, in a mall made up of connected warehouse buildings with very unwarehouse like pillars gracing their fronts. The store sign shines in red neon in the glass window. Evie tells me what to look for and Clare drops me off in front. "When you're done, walk three blocks to the right of the store. We'll find parking in front of the café."

I nod and duck into the shop, spending a few of my precious dollars on a General Equivalency preparation book, complete with sample tests inside. I hesitate near the magazine rack, but change my mind. The prep book is all the reading I'll need until my test is done.

Clusters of tourists and maybe a few locals–their accents part Bronx, part *Gone with the Wind*–brush past me as I make my way toward the café. The far side of the street could be one building, the row houses are so close together, brick to brick, balcony to balcony. Some of them make up one solid building, I realize, with only different styles of the ornate balcony railings to distinguish the businesses. The block falls away at a wide park. A little kid in a windbreaker and old jeans tap dances on the corner for money. Open-topped carriages pulled by long-eared mules with blinders on their temples and flowers on their harnesses stomp the pavement in front of the park. The park itself is more of a plaza. Jackson Square, a sign reads on the black iron gates. Behind it is a white-spired cathedral, fronted by a statue of a man on a horse. Jackson, I'm guessing.

I turn my head to the right. Here, a double set of stairs mount the levee and lead to the river beyond. A brass plaque declares something about the Louisiana Purchase in French and English. Café du Monde is right in front of me.

Built on a wedge of sidewalk at a triangle, the café is mostly open-air, a roof held up by columns with green shades hung between the arches. The awnings are lowered now against the chilly air, but a warm glow leaks out from between the gaps. Clare's station wagon is parked right across the street. Handicapped parking has its privileges, especially in the slow crawl of street traffic that fills this place tonight.

I find Clare and Evie at a table just inside the door. Lamps attached to ceiling fans light the inside of the café and lazily circulate the air. It's warm in here, the breath of dozens of people blowing on their coffee cups. An enclosed room at the back end of the café houses the kitchen and a little gift shop window. I drop down in my seat next to Evie and wait to see what happens.

"How many can you eat?" Evie asks me.

"I don't know. How big are they?" Evie points at a nearby table. A man is stuffing his face with what looks like a three-inch golden brown pillow piled with powdered sugar. A wooden plaque on the wall near the kitchen describes beignets as French doughnuts.

"Three," I decide. The air is sweet with sugar and coffee. I can't wait.

Clare nods. "Three for you, too, Evie? And milk or hot cocoa?"

I stare at the menu, nothing more than a green sticker stuck on the side of the napkin dispenser. "I'd like to try the café au lait, decaf. I've never had coffee with chicory in it before." Chicory was a root the slaves added to leftover coffee grounds to make them go further. Now it's a New Orleans thing, plain and simple. G'ma used to drink it, but she kept me away from coffee. She once told me coffee would darken my skin and stunt my growth. I guess my skin couldn't get much darker, but I did okay on the height thing, so I can't complain too much.

"Me too," Evie says. "Café au lait, regular."

Clare cuts her a smirk. "Oh, yeah, like I'll let you anywhere near caffeine." She flags down a waiter in a green apron and a little paper hat and orders our beignets, with milk for Evie and decaf coffee for the two of us.

We sit in relative silence until the beignets come, then Evie tells me not to inhale before I bite, or I'll choke on the powdered sugar. One bite later, I know she's right. As it is, there's more powder on my jacket than on a ski slope. Evie laughs at me, but it turns out that's just as bad as inhaling, and she goes into a little coughing fit, choking on sugar until it dissolves in her nose and mouth.

"So, what do you think?" she asks me as I polish off the last crumbs.

"Wow. The coffee's weird, kind of bitter, I guess."

"That's the chicory," Clare explains.

"But all in all, it's almost as good as a Wunderbar."

"What's that?" Evie asks.

"A Chicago thing. Cheesecake on a stick."

Clare laughs and Evie wrinkles up her nose. "I'll take beignets any day," she says.

We sip the last of our coffee and milk, listening to the rush of traffic and people laughing, the occasional snatch of jazz from a street saxophone. The shouts of the tap-dancing kid can be heard, and far away, over the levee, the heavy, soft roll of the Mississippi. It's all so good, so familiar, and so strange at once. Suddenly, test or no test, I find myself wishing I had finagled a longer stay.

"And . . . stop." Evie looks up from timing me with the clock. I'm sweating even though it's cool in here, and my hands are shaking.

I drop my pencil. "That sucked."

"Not if you remember what I showed you. It's about logic, not memorization."

"That's what you say, and it made sense when you walked me through it, but . . ." I shrug. "It still sucked."

Evie just smiles and picks up my test. "Do you mind making lunch while I go over this?"

I stare at her, like staring can change all the wrong answers and make them right. Then I dart off to the kitchen. I'm making spaghetti. I wish it was beans and rice, something that would take some time. Anything to keep me from taking more practice tests. But Miss Clare's got a thing for convenience foods. Even the noodles are thin. They take a while, but not long enough.

"Soup's on." Evie's still grading my test. I set the table around her, laying out glasses of iced tea, bowls of spaghetti, and sauce.

Evie looks up at the food. "Thanks. I'm starving." She puts down my test and starts eating.

I laugh, even though it's not funny. "You just gonna eat and leave me hanging?"

Evie smiles, a forkful of spaghetti halfway to her mouth. "You've waited this long. What's a few minutes longer?"

I grab the test. Evie squeals but lets me take it. There's some red on the paper, though not as much as I thought.

"So, this is what I learned in high school."

Turns out I remember most of history. That was my first class in the morning, before G'ma even woke up. I could stay awake through history class just fine. Looks like I'm okay in math, too. Trigonometry stuck with me for some reason, and I took algebra before G'ma got sick. That leaves biology, chemistry, and English, where I'm just barely squeaking by.

"Don't worry, Kendall. All you need to do is pass the test. That's easy."

"For you." I put the test down, and take a bite of my lunch. "At least it'll keep me busy." It's a relief to have something else to think about. Going home to G'ma was the only thing on my mind for almost a year. And then it was finding Aunt Janet. But she's not looking to be found.

That just leaves me and whatever comes next. Life on my own. Quite frankly, I'd rather think about amoebas and chemical symbols.

Evie sees the look on my face and smiles. "You'll pass. If I can do it, I can make you do it."

Words of confidence, if ever I've heard them.

— — —

After a couple more hours of staring at biology questions and Evie getting her own homework done, we decide to head down to Lil' Sam's for a break. I might buy myself that magazine after all. My last purchase before they send me off to the workhouse.

"Hey, Kendall, Evie. Whatchyou doin'?" Marcus asks. I just about jump out of my skin, hands still on Evie's wheelchair.

"Jesus, Marcus. Didn't see you there." He steps out of the shade of the store awning and grins.

"Ha, ha, made you jump," he points at me, grinning. I crack a smile too. It feels good to have something to smile at.

"Hey, Marcus," Evie says softly. I'd swear she sounds shy, but I can't believe it.

"We're going inside." I point at the store with my chin. "Study break."

Inside, I grab a copy of *People* magazine from the rack. Anything that's not a test prep book sounds good to me. Evie pretends to look but doesn't pick anything.

The old man who was behind the counter last time is still there. "Hey, Marcus, you've brought some friends?"

Marcus scampers up to the counter. "Hey, Grandad. This is Kendall. She looks after Miss Clare's little girl." He nods his head toward us.

"Just for the week," Evie and I add automatically. Evie's

voice is even softer and a bit clipped. I don't think she likes being called a "little girl."

"We've met," I add.

"Tell me, did you find Miss Janet?" Mr. Broussard asks.

"No," I admit, and smile weakly. I don't want it to bother me as much as it does.

Marcus is looking at me funny.

"I thought you was taking care of Evie for good."

"No. It's short-term. I'm heading back to Chicago next Wednesday."

Marcus frowns at me but doesn't say anything. I feel like I've lied to him, but if he knew the jam I was in, he'd understand.

"Well, that's not so bad," Mr. Broussard says. "You'll still be here for Mardi Gras."

"Yeah." I nod, and I know I sound wistful. In the middle of the crap storm that is my life, Mardi Gras shines like a lighthouse. It's the stuff of New Orleans legend, the big party my mama always talked about when I was little. The whole world will be rolling with the proverbial good times, while I study and try to figure out the rest of my life. *Laissez les bon temps roules.*

"Hey, Kendall, you got Mardi Gras where you come from?" Marcus pipes in. "Kendall's from Chicago, Grandad."

"Oh, Chi-town. I been up there when I was a young one. Good music and beautiful women in Chicago."

I smile. "No, we don't have Mardi Gras."

"Well, we got it down here. You should come with us to the parades tomorrow."

"Uh . . . sure, if I can. That could be fun." I can't remember the last time I went to a parade. Probably before my parents died.

"And we've got this party we do. It's like a big dance and everything."

I come back to the conversation, hesitant. "I don't do well at parties."

"That's a surprise," Evie practically growls. I'd almost forgotten she was there. My face gets hot. The truth is I've never been to a real party, not since elementary school. Didn't have time for them with G'ma on my hands. Too shy when she wasn't. Not that I was getting many invitations anyway. Except for Hannah's bowling party. And that didn't exactly work out.

"Maybe not Chicago parties," Marcus says, "but this'll be different. It's Friday night. Everybody will be there. And Evie can come too."

"We'd be glad to have you," Marcus' grandad says.

"Thank you, Mr. Broussard."

"No 'Mr. Broussard' here. You can call me Dink."

"Not Sam?" I'm surprised.

"Naw," Marcus says with a big grin. "Sam's my daddy. He used to be smaller than I am now." Mr. Dink winks at me.

"Why, thank you, Mr. Dink," Evie says suddenly. She sounds so sweet, it makes me nervous. "We would love to come."

I put a smile on my face. "Of course. We'll be there."

"Great!" Marcus practically bounces out of his socks.

"Marcus, don't scare those girls away," Mr. Broussard says with a smile.

"Yeah, Grandad, yeah." He holds open the door and I roll Evie out, Marcus on our heels.

Evie hunkers down in her chair, tight-lipped and

moody. "Done yet? Let's go home," she says. Before I can answer, Marcus butts in.

"Dag, Evie. What's your problem, anyway? Kendall's been pushing you around all over the place, and you got nothing nice to say ever."

I'm as startled as Evie, but she reacts first. "Do you know how old I am, Marcus? Seventeen. Seventeen years old. I am not a 'little girl,' or the drooling idiot you made me sound like in there. I'll get into college sooner than either of you, and get a job myself, while I'm at it. So don't make me sound like an invalid."

"Well, you are, aren't you?" Marcus asks. "You've got a handicap."

"Marcus–" I start to say. But he's not asking mean, he's just asking.

Evie must sense the difference too, because she doesn't exactly yell, just purses her lips. "Yes. I'm handicapped. Crippled. Sick. I have seizures and I don't know when they'll happen. And I need help moving from one seat to the next. My hands–" She holds them up to let the shaking speak for itself. "They'll only get worse as I get older." Her voice is hurt now, raw and angry tears quiver in the corners of her eyes. "I'm a shut-in, housebound, and I'll never go anywhere farther than your grandad's crappy little store. So, if that's what you mean by 'invalid,' in-valid, then yes, I am."

She's shaking so hard that her muscle control is falling apart. Her hands spasm and I'm afraid she'll have another seizure right here. I put my hands on her shoulders and try to shush her, but she waves me away, staring defiantly at Marcus. The kid is unflinching.

"My dad's an epileptic. He's got medicine, works at the icehouse across Claiborne. And my grandma's got arthritis so bad, she can hardly pick up a fork sometimes. She's an information operator. Some days she can barely get out of bed." He shrugs. "Heck, Grandad's only had one leg behind that counter since before I was born. But they get by. I bet you could too."

Evie blinks, and the tears finally spill over. She looks down at her lap. My own chest aches for her, for everyone. I'm not the only one with problems, I see.

Marcus raises his eyebrows at me. I shake my head, warning him not to say anything else. I should be angry at him, but I'm not. This is what Clare was talking about. Evie needs to be around people who will tell her how things really are.

"Kendall," Evie says finally. "I want to go home."

I don't argue. "See you later, Marcus."

Marcus stands in the middle of the sidewalk, his jittery arms now limp at his sides, like broken wings. "Bye."

15

Evie's so quiet next door, not even Sarah Vaughan is playing. I'm back to sitting on Aunt Janet's bed, reading the biology test over. But my stomach's so knotted up with worry, I do the only thing I can to distract myself. I drop my test and poke my head through the middle door.

"Hey, Evie. Your mom's not home for a couple of hours. Want a sandwich?"

Evie's in her wheelchair, tapping away at her computer.

"Not hungry," she says, her first words since we got back from the store and she asked to be left alone.

"How about a drink, then? Iced tea?" I come into the room.

Evie sits back and scowls at her monitor. "Not thirsty, either."

I pour us a couple of iced teas anyway and sit in a chair

next to her. She glances at the drink I place on the table but doesn't take it. The monitor lists classified ads. It's probably what I should be looking at too.

"Job search?"

Evie shrugs. I take a chance. "You know, my grandmother once told me that my job was getting my education." Not that I've done a very good job, I realize, but admitting that won't make my point.

This draws a little snort from Evie. "Yeah, well, my mom never even mentions what kind of job my great education is supposed to get me. I've been going for my diploma and going and going. What's next? Online college, grad school? PhD.? My mom'll have me going to school in this little house the rest of my life. I bet I could stay in school forever."

I try to look sympathetic, but I can't. Evie notices.

"Wouldn't that bother you?" she asks.

"Evie, I'm seventeen and I'm nowhere near getting my diploma. The only reason I made it to twelfth grade was my teachers took pity on me. I'm looking at being homeless on the streets of Chicago if I can't make rent in a month. From where I stand, having someone take care of me so I can go to school? That doesn't bother me one bit."

Evie sniffs and looks back at the computer screen. "Yeah, well, some things you can't study at home."

"Like what?"

Evie looks about to say something. Her eyes flicker toward her stereo system, with its wall case of CDs. Instead, she sniffs and gestures with her chin. "At least you can go get your GED. I'll always be in this chair."

"You can do better than that," I challenge. I don't want her blues to be about me.

Evie smirks. "Yeah, I can." She sighs and looks me in the eye, smirk gone. "Do you know what it felt like to hear Marcus rattle off what his epileptic, arthritic old family can do?" Her eyes are big and shining. "He shamed me."

She holds her shaking hands in her lap, head down until a tear falls. She wipes her eyes. "I've got dreams too, you know. But I've been so afraid to do anything, like I'll break if I try, or . . ."

"Die if you fail," I say for her. She looks at me and for a moment we understand each other completely.

"Yeah," she says, and looks away. "Yeah."

My heart feels bruised, but I put a hand on her wheelchair anyway. Now it's my eyes that are starting to tear. "The accident that took my family left me behind in body, but I was so lost. Only my grandmother brought me back. The day the doctors told me she'd had a stroke, it was only knowing that she'd live that kept me going. You said the other day that fear and guilt are stronger than love. Maybe so. I've been afraid to be without love, afraid to figure out who I am without family standing beside me. But they're not around anymore. Not even my stupid aunt." My hand slips off the chair, and tears are falling down my cheeks like rivers, but my voice is steady. She needs to hear this, and so do I. "But you know what? I'm still around. I'm still here." I hold up my hands. They're shaking almost as hard as Evie's. "Not exactly perfect." I even manage a smile. "But I'm working on it. 'Cause, the way I see it, I will really only have failed my family if I fail myself. And that's simply not going to be."

Evie doesn't say anything for a long time. I can hear her breathing, amplified by crying. When she looks up again, the tears are gone, just stains on her cheeks. "I . . ." She takes a deep breath and laughs. "I think I've been feeling sorry for myself."

I rest my hand on her wheelchair again and use the other to dry my face. "I think you have too. But that's your fault, not your mom's. She's just doing what she thinks she has to. If there's something you want, she'll help you get it. If you want to do it on your own, just let her know. You said it yourself–she's devoted to you."

"Devoted." Evie looks like she's tasting the word and it's gone sour.

"So." She looks up at me. "That's part two of your job. Telling me when I'm full of crap. Alma wasn't as good at it as you are."

"Oh, really?" I raise an eyebrow.

"You should keep the job, Kendall," Evie says. "Chicago doesn't sound like home anymore. And . . . after the test, I'd like you to come back to stay."

I study her face. Either she's yanking my chain, or the worm keeps turning here. The latter, I think. It's strange to see.

I look at the keyboard. In my mind's eye, I see Miss Clare and Evie standing on the steps of G'ma's old house with me. I shake the image away, and there's just the keyboard again. Evie's typed away part of the *D,* and the *I* is worn completely off.

"Maybe. Maybe okay."

– – –

When I go back to my side of the house after dinner, there's a letter lying on the floor beneath the front door mail slot. It's a fat envelope, not the junk mail that Janet seems to get daily. I pick it up and see it's addressed to me. My GED application. I fill it out and sign on the dotted line. The test is a few days away, and the sooner I mail it back, the better. Lights are going out in the apartments across the street when I walk to the mailbox outside Maisy Dae's Beauty Parlor. This is my new neighborhood, I tell myself. I like the way it sounds.

16

The telephone wakes me, sending me out of my skin and over the covers. Aunt Janet's phone is ringing. It could be her. It could be anybody. I get off the bed and look at my watch. It's early, not even eight o'clock. I drop to the floor and pick up the receiver.

"Hello?"

"Hi, may I speak to Kendall Washington?" A woman's voice. My heart slams into my throat.

"Speaking," I manage to squeak. My head is pounding in time with my chest.

"Hi, Kendall. May I call you Kendall? My name is Anne Bigford. I'm your case worker, assigned by the state of Illinois."

Not Janet. "Oh. Right." The woman who left the message earlier. "Hi."

"Hi. I've left you a few messages at your Chicago number, and was given this number by your high school today."

"Sorry. I'm visiting my aunt," I lie. "I would've called you."

"That's fine, Kendall. So you are currently staying with your aunt?"

I look around the empty apartment. "That's right. I came down after the funeral. I should've told someone, I guess."

I can practically hear the woman's smile over the phone. "That's all right, honey. Being with family is natural. Unfortunately, it seems there were no provisions made in your grandmother's will."

"G'ma wasn't supposed to die this young," I say. Silence crackles awkwardly down the line.

"Well, the good news is your parents' will indicates that one Janet Wright is your godmother. Is that your aunt?"

It's an effort not to laugh. "Yes."

And my godmother. What a joke. I guess even Mama didn't know her sister too well after all.

"Well, if your aunt is going to take over guardianship, here or in New Orleans, we'll need to speak with her, and there is paperwork to sign."

Before I can worry about how *that's* going to happen, she adds, "The sooner the better, before you're declared truant or a runaway by the state."

"What? I'm not a runaway." There was nothing for me to run from, I want to say.

"I know that, Kendall, and you know that, but the state only sees what's in your file. If your legal guardian is dead, you need a new guardian, or you'll become a ward of the state."

Visions of Oliver Twist dance in my head. "What does that mean?"

The practiced answer is instant, a trained response that makes me wonder how many files like mine she has on that desk of hers. "When a child is left without parents or legal guardian, the state steps in. We'd find a place for you here in Chicago. There are foster situations, and various living facilities. For a girl your age, we might even be able to swing a work/school program that would allow you to pay for your own state-owned apartment while you finish school."

She sounds so pleased when she says it that I almost forget she's talking about sending me to an orphanage.

"See," Ms. Bigford says. "That's not so bad. But you don't need to worry about it, because you have your aunt."

Right.

"So, when will you be back in town?"

"Thursday night." I barely realize I'm speaking. Sleep stuffs my brain. It's too much.

"Great. I've got an opening for Monday, and Thursday. I really don't recommend any later than that."

"Monday's fine," I say, even though it isn't. Between my forged lease and AWOL godmother, nothing's fine anymore.

I hang up the phone and sit there, wishing I could sleep it all away.

"Kendall, you awake?" It's Evie's voice, through the wall. Through my haze of misery, I remember–today is my first parade. Mardi Gras has come to town.

"I'm up, I'm up!" I call back through the wall. Thanks to Ms. Bigford, it's true. My Chicago troubles can wait until I get there. We need to get up early to get a good spot at the parade, according to Marcus. He's going to be here at ten. The parade starts at two. I shake the dreams from my head and hit the showers.

I'm just tying my gym shoes when the bell rings next door. I can hear Miss Clare answer it.

"Hello, Marcus."

"Hey, Miss Clare. My mama made these pralines for you."

"Thank you, Marcus. Evie, entertain our guest. I'll put these in the kitchen."

I stand up slowly and move closer to the adjoining door. I'm dying to hear how Evie and Marcus make up.

"You look nice in purple," Marcus says. He sounds surly, like someone's forcing him to be polite. Not Marcus at all.

"Thanks." Ah, sarcasm. Evie's back to her old self after all. I put a hand on the doorknob, ready to interrupt if it gets any worse.

"You know, I didn't mean to make you mad, Miss Evie," Marcus says abruptly. "You seem like a smart person. You're just mean sometimes."

I stifle a laugh. Honesty, thy name is Marcus.

Fortunately, Evie laughs too. "Got me there. I'll do better next time."

I can practically hear Marcus grin, he sounds so relieved. "Yeah." He chuckles. "Next time. Hey, where's Kendall? We're going to miss all the good spots if we're late."

That's my cue. I take a breath and walk into the room. Evie gives me a look and shakes her head. She knows I've been listening. I smile innocently. "Where's your mom? I'm ready to go."

We pile into the car and head toward St. Charles

Avenue, where the big old American houses are. Today is the Zulu parade, Evie tells me. We're hoping to catch coconuts and fake African jewelry with Zulu written on it in gold. Sounds good to me.

Miss Clare gets us as close as she can to the action, but driving doesn't get you very far in the mass of party people blocking the streets. And what the crowds don't block off, the police do. The place is so jumping, it's almost easy to forget what's ailing me. We give up trying to line up on St. Charles and park in the Garden District near Napoleon. I try to put Ms. Bigford, and the test, out of my mind.

"There." Miss Clare hauls Evie's chair out of the trunk and we roll the last half block to the parade route.

"How come you don't got Mardi Gras in Chicago?" Marcus asks.

I shake off my thoughts and shrug. "How come you've got it here?"

Marcus shrugs back. "My daddy says it's 'cause New Orleans loves a party, so we have one every year."

Clare laughs. "It's true. Only in New Orleans or Rio could they take a church holiday and turn it into a week-long binge."

Evie looks over her shoulder at me. "Mardi Gras ends when Lent starts. That's almost the only time we see the inside of a church, on Ash Wednesday. Sometimes we even give something up until Easter." She pauses. "It's fun. Especially when Mom gives up something essential, like coffee."

Miss Clare swats Evie playfully. Evie fends her off with a raised arm. "The worst forty days of my life. She quits coffee and I start saying my prayers. Isn't that what Lent's all about?"

"Here they come!" Marcus darts ahead to the police

horses blocking the sidewalk from the street. The crowd parts a little when they see Evie's wheelchair. Evie knows it and all but pushes us ahead to make sure we get a good view. Floats, like smaller versions of the ones I've seen on TV in the Macy's Thanksgiving Day Parade, come driving down the street. Signs on all the storefronts shout Mardi Gras greetings. On the floats, women dressed like tribal showgirls in feather headdresses and spangly costume jewelry wave to the crowd. But they're more than waving; they're throwing things.

"Hey, mister! Throw me something!" Marcus yells. "C'mon, Kendall, you gotta yell it or they won't give you nothing."

I feel stupid, until I hear the rest of the crowd shouting along with us. "Hey, mister, throw me something!"

Marcus gets two purple plastic necklaces; I get a cup.

"Kendall, quick!" Evie shouts and points at my feet. A red coin lies on the ground. I reach down to pick it up. "No!"

The guy next to me almost steps on my fingers. I let him have the coin.

"Rude."

"Use your feet," Marcus tells me. "Then your hands. Unless you want to lose your fingers. Dag!"

"Yeah, Kendall." Evie sticks her tongue out at me. "Dag!"

I learn fast. The floats come by quickly, some decorated like undersea treasure coves, some like jungles, with people on board in costume, waving and throwing out trinkets. It's only plastic, I know, but somehow I feel lucky every time I catch something. Marcus even gets his coveted coconut–an ugly little thing covered in glitter and paint that says ZULU.

I get a black comb with ZULU on the handle. Another thing to lose in my hair. Evie's wheelchair turns out to be a necklace magnet. By the time the parade's over, she's got more necklaces than her neck can carry. My throat is hoarse and we're loaded down with so much junk, we look like pirates in a bad movie.

"I caught ten pearl ones," Evie announces proudly. "Plastic or not, pearl beads are the best."

"I got two pearls, and a coconut." Marcus waves his spoils in the air.

"I think I got one of those Popeyes doubloons," I say, squinting at the coin in my hand. Sure enough, the little purple coin advertises a free drumstick at the chicken restaurant.

"Dag," Marcus says, and gives me a high five.

Miss Clare smiles at the three of us. "Had enough? Maybe we can cash in that doubloon for lunch."

"Sounds good to me," I say.

Marcus shrugs. "Sorry. Today's Poor Day. I've got a sandwich in my pocket."

"Poor Day?" Evie asks. "Is that the eighth day of the week?"

"Naw, it's the day before payday for my Momma. I don't get my allowance till tomorrow, and I'm all tapped out."

I hold up a red doubloon. "I caught a few extra Popeyes doubloons, Marcus. I think we can work something out."

Miss Clare wheels Evie around away from the crowd, and we pick our way along the flood of people, back to the car.

We reach the car, and I realize that I feel good. Really,

really good. Good enough to hope. I stop a few steps from the car to figure out what it means.

"Miss Clare?"

She pauses before getting into the car. Evie's already buckled inside, and Marcus is climbing into the back.

"What is it, sugar?"

"I head back to Chicago tomorrow."

"I know. Let's not think about that now."

"I have to go."

"I know."

"But Evie and I were talking, and . . . I'd like to come back. I'd need help to do it, but I'd like to stay."

Suddenly, the crowd goes quiet. Or that's the way it seems to me for the split second before Miss Clare breaks into a grin.

"Well, now, is that a fact," she says. "I think we can work something out with that, too."

17

My brain hurts. It's crammed full of anagrams and easy ways to remember the periodic chart. Evie says they won't ask me to name the whole thing, but if they ask even one, I've got to be ready. Biology was interesting. Chemistry is just plain dry, especially when I can't do any of the experiments the textbooks talk about. No wonder I slept through it.

Harder still is focusing on my test, when all I want to do is clean up my new apartment and run around New Orleans yelling "Throw me something!" Marcus whooped like an Indian in a bad western when he heard I was staying. Evie smiled in a way that made me almost think she had made the decision for me. But I made it myself, and I know it's the right one. I've got this one more subject to study, and then I head to Chicago tomorrow night. When I come back, I'll bring a few things. Enough to start my new life.

But first things first, I've got to study.

"Kendall, break time," Evie says. She pushes back from the table where she's been shuffling a stack of CDs and rolls over to the stereo. Billie Holiday fills the room.

"Just a couple more minutes," I say halfheartedly.

"Ken, the human brain is like a computer. It needs time to process. Stop now. Start later. You'll retain more."

"Fine, fine," I agree, and push the books across the table. "You know, I slept through most of high school. Taking a break now feels like cheating."

Evie rolls her eyes at me and pushes herself over to the refrigerator. "This isn't high school. It's just one test."

"You're right."

She comes back with two cans of soda in her lap. "So, what are you going to wear tonight?"

I rest my head on my hand. "Pajamas."

"Very funny." She hands me a soda. "I meant to the party."

"Party?" A shiver runs up my spine. "Crap, Marcus' party is tonight?"

"Today's Fat Tuesday, isn't it?" Evie hoists her soda in a salute.

I groan and drop my head onto the table. What was it that Hannah Lee said so many days ago? *Wear something cute.*

"I can't do it. I can't go."

"Why not?"

Why not. "I don't know. An entire life spent being

unavailable, not to mention uninvited to parties. I never developed the social muscles. Or the wardrobe, for that matter."

Evie laughs. "Kendall, you are such a drama queen. 'I have nothing to wear!' "

I can't decide whether to be offended or to laugh at my own patheticness. "Well, I don't" is all I say.

Evie opens my soda for me. "Fortunately, Clare does. We'll raid her closet. She'll love it."

"I couldn't," I protest.

Evie fixes me with a look that leaves no room for escape. "You have to."

We settle on an old party dress Miss Clare apparently hasn't worn in years, green with soft black flowers all across it. I don't think it's my color. I don't actually think I *have* a color. I'm hoping I'll just fade into the background. But Evie says it looks good, so I take it back to my side of the house to get ready.

"Kendall, you've been in here for an hour already." Miss Clare appears in the bathroom doorway behind me and shakes her head. I'm dressed, but I've been trying to tame it with my new Zulu comb, and failing. Why couldn't I have been born with good hair? Why did I get the nappy genes?

"Girl, what are you going to do about that hair?"

"I don't know, Miss Clare. This comb is stuck." I show her with a tug. "I look like hell."

I can tell in the mirror Miss Clare's trying not to laugh, but she's laughing anyway. "Aw, Kendall, that's not true. Here. Let's see what we can do."

It takes a little while, and a couple of teeth break off the comb, but she gets it out. So much for my souvenir. "Now,

I've got a wide-toothed comb in my house. Come to the other side and we'll see if we can get this head of yours straightened out and braided."

I have to take my dress off in the end, until she's done. I'm covered with broken bits of hair, and my head's sore as all get-out, but when I look in the mirror, I'm not so ashamed. She's got my hair in two French braids down the sides of my head, and they meet in the back as one braid. A couple of little hair clips add some color to match my dress and the bow in back. It's a miracle. And I tell her so.

"No, it's a bit of patience and determination," she clucks at me. "Now, don't let your head get all out of control like that again!"

"Yes, ma'am." I wash my face, pull the dress back on over my head, and stick my feet into my old black flats.

"Ta-da!" Clare announces me. Evie's been sitting in the living room waiting to see the disaster.

"Well, hallelujah. I was getting worried." Evie's already in her wheelchair, looking chic in a tasteful little black dress with iridescent blue-black trim.

"Fancy getup," I say by way of compliment.

"You don't look so shameful yourself," she says with a smile.

We're standing around grinning stupidly at each other when Marcus knocks on the door. "Hey, Kendall. Miss Clare, Evie." He nods. Marcus is wearing a suit. More like two suits, because the jacket and the pants don't exactly match, and they're too big for him, but he still looks good.

"Wow, Marcus," Miss Clare says.

"You look nice," I tell him. Evie whistles. Marcus blushes.

"I like that dress," he tells me. "You both look nice."

We stand around grinning some more, like fifth graders at a sixth-grade dance. Then I realize Marcus *is* a fifth grader, and I grin even wider.

He is the first to speak. "You ready? Grandad's in the car."

I dump my purse in Evie's lap, put on my coat, and wheel her out the door. "See you in a few hours, Mom," Evie tells Miss Clare. We head outside to where Mr. Dink is waiting in his old town car.

The car is big, but so is Marcus' family. A man sitting in the front seat with Mr. Dink gets out and swings Evie's wheelchair into the trunk. Evie gets deposited in the middle of the backseat, between Marcus and me.

"Just gotta go get my aunt Jo's folks," Marcus tells us confidentially. Aunt Jo's folks are four good-sized people who turn the town car into a sardine can. And then they keep cramming in.

Everybody is one of Marcus' cousins or something. "I don't even think we're really blood-related," he says about some of them. But his family is everywhere. Including my lap. I guess there is such a thing as too much family.

We turn a corner and come to a stop. It takes a lot of squeezing and stepping on people, but we all make it out onto the sidewalk. I smooth out my dress and Evie reappears in her wheelchair looking smushed, but Marcus doesn't even bother to straighten his tie.

"This is it." His eyes have gotten all bright and he's starting to tap his toes, even though I can barely hear the music inside. It's a big old brick building, one story, the kind of place old people rent to play bingo. But tonight there's a man the size of a gorilla standing outside checking tickets, and a line as long as the Mississippi, full of people in masks and fancy clothes, all waiting to get in. Much snazzier than a bowling alley party back home. I say a silent thanks to Miss Clare for getting my hair right.

"C'mon, Miss Kendall, Miss Evie," Mr. Dink says, leaving his car for someone else to park. He holds a cane in one hand and takes me by the arm. Marcus grabs Evie's wheelchair, and we cut to the front of the line.

"Evening, Mr. Dink," the gorilla at the door says.

"Evening, Howie. This here is Miss Evie Morreal and Miss Kendall Washington. And you remember my boy's son, Marcus."

"Hey, Marcus, how's it going?" Howie the Gorilla gives us a nod and Marcus a handshake that looks more like a high-five slap.

"S'all right," Marcus nods, looking two years old when he does it. I have to smile.

"Sir, you can go right in." Howie opens the door, and that music I could barely hear a minute ago hits us like a Chicago wind. Jazz. Mardi Gras.

I catch my breath, and we go inside.

18

Someone at the door tosses a purple feather boa around my neck. "For the lady," a man says. A woman gives me a little cardboard hat that says MARDI GRAS on it. Evie's given a bright yellow boa and a green foil tiara. The room is decorated like a high school party, with purple, green, and yellow balloons all over the place, and colored lights flashing. But the band is far from high school–it's making the whole room jump. Up onstage, a man with a voice like Louis Armstrong sings. All around the room, women in slinky dresses and evening gowns, wearing masks or feathers in their hair, dance in a line with men in suits and even tuxes. Everybody's singing a song about New Orleans. I wish I knew the words, because it makes you want to sing along.

"C'mon, Kendall!" Marcus yanks me away from his grandad and we are swept up into the dance line. I reach out to Evie, but we're halfway across the room before I can even touch her hand. She waves me away with a laugh and disappears in a swirl of bodies.

One thing about me, I can't dance. Another thing–neither can Marcus. But it doesn't matter tonight. We dance with everyone past the band, where people on the edges of the stage throw beads down to us. Everybody waves their hands in the air, catching the necklaces as they fall. Evie's made her way closer to the band, her lap full of beads. I wave to her, but she's so into the music, she doesn't see me as we dance on by. One song later, I'm covered in party jewelry, and happy as I've ever been in my life.

"Want something to drink?" I nod and Marcus pulls me toward the bar, which is really just a punch table with a woman standing behind it.

"What'll you have, honey?" she asks me.

"Pineapple soda?" I don't have to ask twice. They have everything here.

I drink two sips, catch a glimpse of Evie nodding her head to the music, and then we're back in the dance line again. I'm starting to learn at least the choruses to some of the songs, so I can sing along too.

"Mr. Dink, looks like Marcus has got his hands full," the lady behind the punch table says to Marcus' grandaddy when we dance by again.

I turn around and realize I haven't actually seen Marcus for a couple of songs. And then he comes pushing through the crowd with a couple of paper plates in his hands.

"Kendall, you've gotta try this!"

"What is it?" We pull ourselves out of the tug of the crowd and around to the safety of the punch table.

"King cake." He shoves a plate at me.

It looks like nothing I've ever seen before, a big loaf of braided bread covered in colored sugar crystals, three big swaths in the Mardi Gras colors.

"The purple's for justice, green's for faith, and gold's for power," Marcus tells me.

I take a bite. "Thanks–ow!"

"What?" Marcus pulls his face from his plate long enough to watch me fish around in my mouth.

"I bit into something. . . . This." It's a pink plastic baby doll. "A toy." I feel sick. I can see some sticky little kid dropping this into the batter. Gross.

"Aw, man!" Marcus screams. "You got the doll!"

"Hey, congratulations," Mr. Dink says, and winks at me.

"What for? Do I get a prize if I find a roach in the punch, too?"

"Naw, man! That's the baby doll!" Marcus shouts, kicking the floor. "It's good luck. They bake one into every king cake. Man! I never get the doll! And I'm starting junior high next year!"

I can't help but smile. This good-luck doll is a nasty-looking little thing, with a toothmark where the little forehead curl should be, and bits of chewed-up cake stuck all up under its arms.

"Marcus, if it means that much to you, you can have it." I hold it out to him. "Let me just suck some of that cake off for you; it'll be good as new."

Marcus gives me a disgusted look. "Dag!" He waves his arm in my face and walks away, tossing his slice of cake into the trash. I laugh so hard, I drop the rest of my cake into my punch. So much for the good-luck doll. But then again, Marcus must've seen it happen, because he's laughing at me too.

"Let's get some for Evie," he says. We cut her a slice, but before we can even look for her, the lights go dim.

"Blackout?" I ask. Marcus shrugs. Next to us, Mr. Dink just smiles.

"There's your little friend, there." He points to the stage. Two men are lifting Evie and her wheelchair onto the stage. I feel my hands get sweaty and I don't know why.

The band has stopped playing. The dance floor winds to a stop, like a music box. All eyes are on Evie. She wheels herself to the microphone. Her hands are shaking a little more than usual. My own heart's beating like I'm the one onstage. I try to catch her eye, figure out what's going on, but she's staring straight ahead at the mike. And then I get it.

Evie grabs the mike hard, doesn't fumble it once. Puts it to her lips. And starts to sing.

She's got a voice like dark chocolate, sweet, bitter. Smoky. It's got no business being in the body of a girl her age. Everybody knows it. You could hear a pin drop. There's only Evie and a hundred pairs of ears waiting to hear her. All at once, the audience sways to the left, and the band joins in–saxophone, piano, trumpet. I know the song. One of her favorites. Sarah Vaughan's version of "Stormy Weather." *Don't know why there's no sun up in the sky . . . stormy weather.*

The sway turns into a step, turns into a slow dance. Marcus and I just stand there, slack-jawed, stunned. Evie Morreal is a vocal knockout.

She ditches her slouch, rises up in her chair, pulling herself forward with the microphone until, even though she's still sitting, she seems six feet tall. That crazy-rich voice filling the room with enough blues to fill an ocean. I want to clap. I want to cry. I want Miss Clare to hear this.

And then the song ends and she's done. The lights come up a little, and everyone's screaming and whistling, but nobody louder than Marcus and me.

Evie flushes, like the spirit has just left her, and she's slouching, sour-faced Evie again. She puts the mike away, now with quaking hands. The trumpet player wheels her to the edge of the stage, shakes her hand, and helps the men lower her back to earth.

Marcus and I can't get to her fast enough. She's surrounded by backslappers and smiling faces when we finally push through.

"What the hell was that?" I call out to her, tripping over someone. I catch myself on the arm of her wheelchair and settle into a crouch beside her.

Evie's sweating and grinning and blinking like she just woke up. But she doesn't say a word. Marcus grabs her shaky hand and pumps it up and down.

"Hoo-*wee,* Miss Evie. You got a voice on you like something else! I bet you could sing with the band for real every night, with a voice like that."

Evie's shocked face finally wakes up. "You think so?"

"Why, sure." Marcus nods vigorously. "Everybody likes you."

Evie suddenly looks tired. She turns to me. "Kendall? I think I need something to drink."

I hand her my pineapple soda. "Come on, we'll get more." We wheel her over to the bar.

"Jesus, Evie, why didn't you tell me you could sing?" I ask once we all have fresh drinks in our hands. The band's playing again, a bouncy song, and the party's moving along. The three of us are taking a time-out on a bench by the king cake table.

Evie laughs nervously, her eyes on her lap. "I'm surprised you haven't heard me."

My eyes narrow. "I heard you, all right. I thought it was a CD."

Evie blushes. When she looks up again, her face seems really young. "At home with the stereo is one thing . . ." She shrugs. "But Clare would've never let me do it for real."

"How do you know?" Marcus asks.

"Has she ever even heard you sing?" I want to know.

Evie shrugs, uncomfortable with the question. "Mom thinks that too much excitement can bring on a seizure. Singing live is . . . exciting."

We all three break into grins. "Got that right," Marcus says.

I shake my head. "Damn. Evie Morreal, lady sings the blues."

Evie's grin turns into a shy smile. "Hey, Marcus, can your one-legged, arthritic, cross-eyed cousin do that?"

Marcus looks her straight in the face and says, "Naw, man, Billy can't carry a tune worth salt. He's a pretty good dancer, though."

— — —

I'm still singing to myself when Mr. Dink drops us off after midnight. Marcus is snoring on my left. On my right, Evie's silent, like all the sound's gone out of her since she left the stage. The lights are off in Evie's side of the house. Miss Clare never guessed we'd be home this late. Then again, neither did we.

"Time for bed, songbird." I wheel Evie into the house. Her mother's asleep on the couch. She wakes up when we come in.

"Hey, kids, how was it?"

I look at Evie, but she's keeping quiet. Like if she opened her mouth, all the good feeling might slip right out. Miss Clare sees that look and nods.

"That good, huh?"

I smile. "Yeah. That great."

"Don't forget church tomorrow," Miss Clare reminds me.

I say good night, slip through the side door, and feel my way toward the bed. I'm tired as a dog, but it was worth every last dance step. "Mardi Gras mambo, mambo, mambo . . ." I hum myself to sleep.

19

"Hey, Miss New Orleans."

Evie smiles proudly at me from beneath a ridiculously big sunflower hat. "Welcome to the South, Little Miss Chicago," she says to me. "You'd do well to wear a hat too."

I shake my head and laugh to hold back a bushel of sad feelings. "You sound like my grandmother. Completely ignoring the fact that I have a nineteen-hour bus ride ahead of me."

"Details," Evie says, gracing me with a smile. She calls over her shoulder, "Ready when you are, Mom."

"Just a minute, ladies." Miss Clare sticks her head out of the bathroom, still pulling hot curlers out of her hair. "Kendall, go on and put your bag in the trunk. We're late as it is." She comes toward us zipping her skirt, jams a foot into her high heels, and snatches the hat off Evie's head all at once.

She pats herself down. "That's better."

I grab my duffle and meet them out on the sidewalk.

"Shoot, forgot my uniform." Miss Clare runs back inside. I drop my bag in Evie's lap and roll her to the car.

Evie is humming "Stormy Weather." Last night is so fresh on her, I don't have the heart to say anything about Ms. Bigford. Instead, I ask about her.

"Hey, you tell your mom about last night yet?"

Evie shakes her head. "No."

"Why not?"

Evie just shrugs. If I didn't know better, I'd say she was scared of something.

"That's all you've got to say?"

"No, it's not." She twists in her chair to look at me. "She'll either say I shouldn't overexert myself or push me to sing for the opera. She can only push or put down. Last night was too perfect to let her ruin it this morning."

Maybe it's because I've got so much ahead of me. Or maybe it's because of Aunt Janet and every little thing I've been through since G'ma died, but suddenly Evie's teen angst sounds like a two-year-old's crying. And I let her know it.

"You are so full of crap," I say, just this far from yelling it. We're wedged in the open doorway of the car, with only a foot of space between us. "Do you ever listen to yourself?"

Evie blinks, and says nothing. I keep going.

" 'Waa, waa, waa. Life's so damned hard.' Marcus was right. You're a big baby, Evie. You don't deserve to be treated any better than one."

I don't know if she's going to yell, or cry, or just stare at me. I don't wait. I bend down and haul her out of the chair faster than I should. She's heavier than she looks, and she's not helping me one bit.

I'm rougher than I mean to be when I buckle her seat belt. We knock foreheads, and little stars dance in my eyes.

"Crap."

"Jesus, Kendall, what's wrong with you? I thought we were friends."

I'm about to say something brusque, but that stops me short. We are supposed to be friends. I stand back from the car and rub my forehead.

"Forget it," I say. "I just . . ." I shake my head. I want to get on that bus and get out of here. I want to get the next few days over with. Like a book you read the end of first so you can find out what happens. Until then, there's nothing to talk about.

"Let's go, let's go!" Miss Clare rushes out of the house, shoving an earring into her ear. Evie and I break our stare. I hop into the passenger side, rubbing my forehead, and we're off. A breeze washes by. Neither of us says another word.

— — —

Church in New Orleans is something else. Back in Chicago, we only sang when we were supposed to, and the only person who got to talk was the minister. Down here, the music's different and it seems like everybody's talking and the minister likes it that way.

On top of it all, Ash Wednesday's not like a regular service. Instead of a sermon, today is mostly about standing in line to get in and get blessed with palm ashes. Even though

Evie says her wheelchair is usually an automatic cut to the front of the line, this morning we have to wait for our blessings. She's not the only person here in a wheelchair.

The minister stands behind the pulpit, talking and praying, and the band plays soft, floaty, holy-sounding music as we inch forward to the altar. Once there, Miss Clare and I get to drop down to our knees on either side of Evie and say our pre-Lent prayers.

I pray for G'ma and Mama, and Daddy and Little Mackie. I pray for luck on my GED test. I pray to be a better person than I just was to Evie, and for Evie to be better to herself. And I ask God to tell me what I'm supposed to do come Monday morning in Chicago. Even with Miss Clare's help, it might not work. I pray for luck. Instead, I get the press of the minister's finger on my forehead, and a cool brush of palm leaf ash. It feels soft on my bruised skin.

"Amen." I stand up again and leave the altar. Miss Clare and Evie have already left it. They're waiting for me at the door.

"You all right, Kendall, honey?" Miss Clare asks. Evie avoids looking at me.

I nod. I hadn't realized I'd been there that long. "Yeah," I lie.

Miss Clare smiles and gives me a hug. "Come on. We'll take you to the station."

20

The sky over Chicago is dark blue when my bus pulls in. I've pulled the all-day version of an all-nighter, too rattled to do more than shut my eyes. I sleepwalk the three blocks to the L station, my brain humming like it's recovering from novocaine. Chicago, Chicago, my kind of town. It doesn't feel real. The air is cold, wind blowing off the river. It smells like it might have rained earlier, but it's not cold enough to snow.

My legs are numb by the time I reach my block. The brownstone is there, just like it should be. I stand on the doorstep and get a sudden chill. It's not so good to be home again.

I fumble with the keys, unfamiliar after twelve days of disuse, and finally step inside. It's dark in the hallway, the radiator hissing in the corner. The place smells thick with memories, like old fruit. Sweet, but so far gone, it'll make you sick. I place my hand on the banister and realize how much I don't want to be here. I don't want to spend another night in our house without G'ma. I don't want to smell her smells and feel her missing. For a minute I think about a motel. But it's like New Orleans. I don't have the money. Where else am I supposed to go?

I grip the banister and haul myself up the stairs. I take one step, then another. I'm missing G'ma's hand on mine, squeezing tight while she clutches the rail on the other side. Easing her way, step by painful step, up to the apartment. I stop on the landing, where she used to stop to catch her breath. And I catch my own. I didn't think it would be this way. Coming home shouldn't be hard. Just focus on the test, I tell myself. That's what I'm here for. After that, it's out of my hands.

I open the apartment door and take a startled breath.

"G'ma." I can smell her, like faded flowers or some kind of good food in a neighbor's kitchen. I drop my bag, shut the apartment door behind me, close my eyes, and inhale to the bottom of my lungs. God, I miss her. Miss her like I'd miss my own heart. G'ma, G'ma.

I've got a hurt in my stomach that sits up high, just beneath my ribs. I open my eyes and make my way down the hall, past the sofa I camped on all those nights, to G'ma's dim little bedroom, still the same way she left it. I set the alarm clock to 6:30 a.m., and I drop down onto the bedspread, curl myself around the pillows like they're her lap and fall fast asleep.

— — —

Chicago hasn't changed one bit. The L still rattles with the same back-and-forth motion, past the clotheslines and blond brick walls of the row houses in Rogers Park. It's Friday morning in March. The sky looks like a painting, blue and white with fluffy little clouds. There's still snow crusting the ground where shadows lie. You can smell it, sharp and wet, beneath the oily scent of bus exhaust and almost-bitter road salts. My fingers are cold, but all I have in my book bag are pencils and a calculator. I left my gloves at home.

The train stops and I walk the few blocks to Harry Truman College, where I'll take the biggest test of my life.

The hallways smell like rubbing alcohol and bleach. Like the halls of G'ma's hospital. I try not to think of it, my gym shoes squeaking on the shiny granite floor as I follow the signs to the lecture hall where the test will be. A woman is sitting outside. She wears a name tag that reads Proctor. Pretty name, I start to say, but it's a lame joke.

"Hi, are you here for the GED?" she asks. Her hair is strawberry blond, in a flippy sort of bob that is way too young for her forty-year-old freckled face. The rest of her is hidden in a turtleneck sweater the color of oatmeal.

"Hi. Yes, my name is Kendall Washington."

The proctor lady runs down the crappy computer printout sheet of registered test-takers, mumbling, "Washington, Washington." I look around to see who else is here. There are more women than men. Two women that sound like girls, both dressed in sweatpants and overcoats, are laughing behind their manicured hands. One of them has a tiny gold stud in her nose. Across the hall, coming out of the bathroom, is a man who could be somebody's grandfather. He's got salt and pepper in his day-old beard. I bet someone's making him take this test. He puts his hands in his jacket pockets and heads into the testing room.

"I'm sorry, but I don't see you down here."

"What?" My attention snaps back to the proctor in front of me. I look at her list. "Could you check again? The secretary at my school signed me up last week. She said it would be no problem. Kendall Washington. Kendall, with a *K*."

The woman scans the sheet again, and turns it around to show me. "Sorry, dear. Oh. Hold on. There were a few people we had problems with. . . ." She reaches into a briefcase beneath the table.

"Here. Oh, Kendall Washington, right. There's a note for you here. It looks like your registration was rejected. As a minor, your application needs to be signed by a parent or legal guardian."

Lightning strikes me, sticks me to the spot. "What?"

I think back to the night the papers came. I'd filled them out so quickly, and I didn't have to forge Janet's name. "No," I tell the proctor. "The application said I just had to be a minor who is out of school, and I am."

The proctor shakes her head. "This happens more often than you'd think. You have to have been out of school for at least a year, or else you need your guardian's signature. Has it been a year?"

I stare at the proctor, but I'm not seeing her. I could only see red.

The proctor lady looks at me and purses her lips. "I know this must be disappointing for you. I'm so sorry the school didn't tell you. They must've sent a letter, though." A letter that came after I left, mailed to my aunt's address. I feel sick. The proctor flips through the stack of papers and hands me a sheet.

"These are the requirements. Apparently, you're not

quite eighteen yet? Oh, a birthday in two months. That's my sister's birthday. Happy birthday." She smiles at me and the look I give her withers the grin.

"Right, well, in Illinois, unless you are eighteen, you have to have been out of school for at least a year. Or in the military. Or–"

"Prison?" I read the form out loud. "A ward of the Department of Corrections or an inmate?"

"Or pregnant . . . ," the lady says lamely. "You're not pregnant, are you?"

I almost wish I was. Before I can stop them, hot tears fill my eyes. I dash them away and throw the application back on the table. There, right at the bottom, is the place where Aunt Janet's signature should have been.

The proctor hands me a tissue from her bottomless briefcase. "Look, maybe you can talk to your school on Monday. I'm sure they can help you figure something out."

Right. Monday.

Monday.

I drop my book bag and leave it at the test site, number two pencils and all.

Instead of going back to G'ma's apartment, I go to the cemetery where my family is buried. This is the closest thing to home I've got left in Chicago now.

The gates are open, but no one's around. The mausoleum's quiet. I guess nobody died today. I cross the lawn with its perfect grass and smooth-paved pathways to the willow that shades my family's headstones. I huff my way over the rise, to the little man-made hill where my grandmother lies under the ground, next to the rest of my family.

The grass over G'ma's grave is greener than the rest, like a grass rug laid over a green floor.

The whiplike branches drape a curtain of green over us, just the five of us, four headstones and me.

I hate my family.

I haul back my foot and kick, hard and square at the headstone that says Louisa Ella Wright, kicking at the fresh-cut stone with its shiny new end date. G'ma planned her own funeral, including buying her own headstone, but she didn't plan a damn thing for me.

I kick and scream and tear at the branches above me.

I collapse on top of my grandmother's grave.

21

Everybody's singing.

Everybody's singing except for Mama. She's driving us home. Daddy's waving his fingers in the air like a music man, a train conductor, and we are singing with him. "A knife and a fork and a plate of beaaans," we sing. "That's how you spell New Or-leeeeans!"

"That's right. That's one thing. Now do the other one," Daddy tells us. I squeeze Mackie's hand. He's in a car seat, but I'm a big girl. I can undo my car seat. I do it because Mackie's not allowed to.

"Come on, Kenderella, sing us the one about home."

Mackie doesn't know the words, but I do. "A chicken and a car and the car won't goooo, that's how you spell Chi-ca-go!"

"Slow down, now, Ginnie. There's ice out there you

can't see," Daddy says to Mama. It's snowing outside. Our windows are foggy and cold.

"I know that, James. Don't you think I know that? But we've wasted enough time down here. I want to get home." Mama's voice is funny. Tight, like mine is when I fall off the swings and hurt myself.

"Mama, does it hurt?" I ask her.

Mama looks at me in the mirror and smiles. "I guess it does, sweetie. But that's okay. That's okay. Now, why don't you sing me another song? Something longer. How about that one about the bird?"

"It's not a song, Mama. It's a rhyme. Songs have singing."

"Well, then do the rhyme for us, sugar belle."

"I saw a little bird on the window go hop, hop, hop. I said, 'Little bird, won't you stop, stop, stop?' "

I forget the rest of the words because the car goes funny, and Mama stops smiling in the mirror at me. Daddy holds out both hands, like a football man, not a music man, and Mackie stops squeezing my hand. Mackie starts to cry, so I cry too.

"Virginia," Daddy says. And I look out the window, and the trees on the side of the road go around us, and around, and around. The trees are pale and frosty, like Christmas cookies.

I hear a sound, like boots through snow, but louder, so much louder. My door comes undone and I go through it. I'm not wearing my car seat, like Mackie. I'm a big girl. I can see our car. It's Daddy's favorite. White, with painted-on wood. The car looks broken.

I see sky. I see trees.

22

I see trees. Broken willow branches. I sit up slowly, my head sore, my leg throbbing. The sight of my grandmother's shattered grave makes me feel sick. I start to stand up, when I hear the squawk of a walkie-talkie.

"Don't move." A security guard is standing a few yards away, nightstick in his hand, pointing at me. He grabs his radio. "Yeah, we found someone. It's a real mess. I'll bring her in."

— — —

Whatever you've seen of jail on TV, it's not what you think. The walls are pink in here. Not pink like bubble gum, but like the life's been taken out of the color. Even the bars that make the rest of the cell up are painted that same tired color. I sit down on the bench jutting out of the wall, and hang my head.

I didn't hear that security guard coming. I don't know that I would've run away if I had. Too busy lying on G'ma's broken grave, head in the dirt, hands in the grass, sobbing until I dried myself out. And now I'm waiting. Waiting for them to figure out that I don't have any parents coming to bail me out. No money for a lawyer, either. They haven't even said I can call someone. Even if they did, I wouldn't know who to call. I'd rather stay here forever than tell Miss Clare and Evie what I've done. I guess I'll just stay here and rot.

"Miss Washington." A woman's voice, making a statement, not a question. I start, then immediately brush back my hair, the four-day-old braids Miss Clare gave me come undone in a burst of knots. I don't need a mirror to know I look like crap. So I pull my hair back the best I can, and look up.

A white woman in a camel-colored wool coat and pantyhose stands in front of me, her hand on the strap of a burgundy leather briefcase.

"Are you my lawyer?" They'd promised me a free lawyer if I couldn't afford one. The woman smiles.

"No," she replies, walking up to my cell. "Much worse. I'm your social worker. Anne Bigford. We have an appointment on Monday?"

She reaches her hand through the bars, offering a shake. I hesitate, a flash of hot embarrassment blazes my face. Monday.

"I'm so sorry," I say.

"Kendall, please." Her tone makes me look at her. She's not angry, just trying to shake my hand. After a second, I stand up and comply.

"So," she says. "You want to tell me what's going on?"

We stand there, her handprint still warm against my palm, and size each other up. From the top of her pale blond head to the bottom of her leather pumps, I've never seen this lady before, and yet she's got my entire life in her hands. And, I decide, whether on Monday or today, the truth is going to come out sometime.

"What's going on," I repeat. I turn my cheek and rest it on the cool pink bars. "It's the breakdown of the American family, Ms. Bigford." I look her in the eye. "I lied to you about my aunt."

She cocks an eyebrow. "I see. And what about New Orleans?"

This time, I can't hold eye contact. "I went down to find her, and instead I found out she ran away. From me. Can you believe it?" My fists clench around the bars of the cell. If I had the strength, I'd tear them out of the walls and throw them at the memory of Janet.

Instead, I try to explain. "I didn't know what else to do, so I lied. But then I met some people down there. Some really good people. And my school said I could take the GED, and I thought, 'Well, that's something, at least.' " I choke on my laugh. Better than nothing. "It was more than that. It was good. Really good."

Ms. Bigford shakes her head. She leans back against the far wall, her arms folded across her chest. Her blond-gray hair bounces with disapproval.

"So why the vandalism?"

I blanche and my eyes grow wet. "It wasn't . . . it's not what it looked like. I was angry. I was . . ." I look up at the social worker, at a loss for the right words. "Did I break anything?"

Ms. Bigford doesn't spare me a kind smile. Instead, she

steps forward again and unfolds her arms. "What are you angry at, Kendall?"

Just like that, I feel sapped of strength. I back up and sit down on the little cell bench. "The GED people, for one thing. I couldn't take the test without my aunt signing off on it. Like I don't exist, can't make my own decisions without her."

"So you vandalized your grandmother's grave?"

The words are ugly. Something inside me breaks loose, just as ugly and mean.

"Yes," I snap. "So I vandalized my grandmother's grave. The grave of the only woman who ever gave half a damn about me. Missed her so much I thought I'd dig her up."

Ms. Bigford doesn't blink. I do.

"What do you want from me, Ms. Bigford. An apology? Well, how about an apology to me, too? How about an 'I'm so sorry, Miss Washington, but you fell through the cracks. If only we'd done our jobs sooner, you would be taken care of right now'? Where were you and your files when my grandmother's Medicare wouldn't pay for a day nurse? When I had to skip school to take care of her, and was *still* making good grades? I was a freaking Eagle Scout, and you were nowhere. But the minute I slip up, the minute I need more than a handshake and some sympathy, I end up here? On second thought, Ms. Bigford, I'm not sorry at all. You should be sorry. You and every single person out there that says I'm too old to be a kid, too young to be on my own, and too damned unimportant to read the file on until three weeks after my whole world ends."

Ms. Bigford looks me dead in the eye. "I am sorry," she says. "I'm sorry that yours is not the only file in the world."

If the door was open, I'd slam it. Instead, I turn my back and stand in a corner, willing Ms. Bigford to go away.

By some small miracle, she does. But not for long. And when she returns, she's got an attendant with her who unlocks my cell with a long set of jangling keys.

I stand in my corner, looking out. I don't know what to do.

"Come on," Ms. Bigford says. "You look like a pound puppy in there."

I don't like the comparison, but I can't disagree.

"Are you taking me to an orphanage?"

Ms. Bigford gives me a considering look. "It's all about choices, Kendall. That's only one of them. What do you want?"

"To find my aunt." I say it automatically. I don't even think I mean it anymore. My voice cracks on the words, tired of making the same old sounds. "No," I say quickly. "Not that."

"Then what? We can help find her, if you want. What do you want?"

What do I want? It's been twelve days since G'ma died, and already I'm in jail and a high school dropout, with no idea of how to get out of this mess. G'ma's not here to help me anymore, and Aunt Janet's not coming to fill in. Miss Clare said she'd help, but she's got her hands full with Evie. What can she do? What can anyone do? Now I've got the city willing to help me bring her home.

"I'm supposed to find my aunt," I say, more to myself than to anyone else. "It's what G'ma wanted. She asked for Janet at the end. My aunt should know that."

Ms. Bigford nods but says nothing. She lets me finish what I have to say.

"But the thing is, I'm tired of looking. There's never been anyone who didn't want to be found as much as Aunt Janet. I get that. I get the message. So, at what point can I just leave it alone? When does family stop being the only reason to keep going?"

Ms. Bigford doesn't even shrug. She just says, "So, what do you want to do?"

I sigh and take a step toward the door. I feel G'ma's ghost shuffling behind me, and Mama and Daddy, and baby Mackie, too. I feel the whole clothesline of baptismal gowns that make up my relations tying me back to the family tree. I love you, Mama. I love you, Daddy. I love you, Mackie, and G'ma, too. But you left me on my own and that's what there is now.

I let go of the bars and Aunt Janet all in one breath.

"Ms. Bigford, I just want to be free."

23

Somebody's singing a spiritual. Somebody's singing that old song for all they're worth. "A band of angels coming after me, coming for to carry me home." The words echo, sweet and sorrowful through the bus terminal. Halfway between bathroom tile and garage noise, the music echoes. The singer is a woman, huddled in a pile of old clothes, leaning up against the depot wall, cup out, eyes down, singing for her supper. I step off the bus and walk toward her, toward the door to the terminal.

"Swing low, sweet chariot," the woman sings. I fumble in my pocket for a crumpled dollar bill, find a five instead, and put it in her cup. The woman nods, but doesn't really look at me. It could've just been part of keeping time. I pass through the glass doors, the song still playing melancholy in my ears. "I looked over Jordan, and what did I see, coming for to carry me home?"

Evie is at the far end of the station, waving at me. I smile back. Miles fall off me like melting snow. The thin crowd shifts, and I can see Miss Clare standing near her daughter. Until now, I didn't realize I was frowning. I've been gone so long, and now I've got people waiting for me. Waiting to take me home.

"So, how was it?" Miss Clare asks. She gives me a hug with one arm, and reaches for the hatbox with the other hand. "Here, let me carry that."

"Oh, no." I pull the box out of reach. "These are for Evie." I drop the box in Evie's lap. She clutches it, trying not to smile. "Used to be G'ma's."

Evie loses the fight and smiles at me. "Just what I need, a place to put my Sunday hat–but it's heavier than that."

I wink at her. G'ma's lonely-day records might feel a little less alone in New Orleans. "Open it at home."

She nods and we wheel our way out to the car. Miss Clare's doing this on her lunch break. We head off in a rush.

The story of the rest of my trip spills out on the ride home. "Seven weeks, and the judge finally emancipated me."

"As in the Emancipation Proclamation?" Evie asks.

I think back to the woman singing at the station, songs the slaves sang in hopes of being freed. "Yep. With your written testimony, Miss Clare, and affidavits from my grandmother's doctor and my school, the court agreed to recognize me as an adult, even though I'm not eighteen. And Ms. Bigford said seven weeks was fast. Because my job was down here, any longer would have been considered a hardship.

"Now I can take care of myself. I can work and live on

my own, without a guardian. And, best of all, in Louisiana, it means I can take the GED when it comes up again next month."

"Good for you, Kendall," Miss Clare says, and flashes me a smile in the rearview mirror.

"Yes, bully for you," Evie says sarcastically, but she's smiling too. "Does this mean you won't bash me in the head anymore?"

I laugh. "Only if you deserve it."

Miss Clare shakes her head. "Then I guess we'd better buy you both helmets."

I smile and sit back into my seat and watch New Orleans roll by. "It's been a strange couple of months."

"Well, you're home now," Miss Clare replies as we pull up in front of the house. "You can freshen up, unpack, and relax. We can all have a celebration dinner tonight, catch up on the details of your trip. And tomorrow, you and Evie can start putting that apartment together the right way."

"Yes ma'am," I agree, grinning. Life goes on, and I'm going along with it.

We pile out of the station wagon and haul Evie back into her chair, still clutching G'ma's hatbox full of records. We're halfway up the walk when the wrong thing happens. The door to my apartment opens from the inside. A woman steps out, frowning, and turns to lock the door. Miss Clare is the first to speak.

"Janet?"

I freeze, my heart slamming against my chest jackhammer hard. Everything else has gone so quiet, I could scream.

The woman turns around, angry words on her lips. "Clare Morreal, how dare you throw away my things–"

Her eyes land on Clare, then shift to me. Her face changes from righteous to . . . If I didn't know better, I'd say that look was fear. She takes a half step toward us like testing pool water with her toe, then stops and gives me a sad, shaky little smile I recognize. Mama's smile. I blink hard.

"Aunt Janet."

She holds out her hands to me.

"Kennie, sweetie. Hello."

24

Her nose is too thin and her skin too caramel-colored to be Mama's. Mama was like chocolate. Janet just looks . . . weird. I want to tell her to get out from behind my mama's smile, but it's been so long since I've seen it, I'm walking toward her before I can stop myself.

"I thought you were gone," she says so softly, I almost don't hear her. Then I'm standing in front of her and she says, "Dear God, it's been so long." She wraps her arms around me. She smells like lavender and sweat. It's a nervous smell, the kind that means your deodorant is running out.

"Now, let me look at you." She pushes me back, holds me at arm's length with a little laugh. I'm taller than her. And overdressed. Aunt Janet's wearing a frayed lilac-colored V-neck sweater and old washed-out jeans. G'ma would've called them tacky, at-home clothes. And suddenly I feel sick. I pull out of her grasp.

Her eyes tear up, and I can't tell if it's fake or not. "Oh, Kendall, honey, I'm so sorry I couldn't make it to the funeral. My car broke down a day outside of the city. I . . ." She falters, puts her hand on my shoulder again and looks past me to Miss Clare and Evie.

"Thanks for looking out for my niece here, Miss Clare. Looks like you've been taking good care of her."

I've never seen Miss Clare and Evie look as much alike as right now. Their faces are set hard, arms folded tight across their chests. Evie snorts in disgust.

"I didn't do any favors for you, Janet," Miss Clare says. "Kendall's earning her own keep around here. She's my new boarder. I'd write you a check for your deposit, but the state you left the place in will all but chew it up."

Aunt Janet laughs nervously. "Well, Miss Clare, here I am, back to make things right. I just had a little car trouble is all."

Miss Clare shakes her head. Evie's grinding her jaw so hard, I can hear it. Her eyes burn into my aunt's head.

My aunt. My mother's sister. She's standing right here. With me. Family.

Aunt Janet is the first to speak. "Y'all going to just stand here, or are you going inside?"

I blink, and fumble for my house key. But Miss Clare doesn't budge. She and Evie exchange a look.

"I'm sorry, Kendall, but your aunt is no longer welcome in our house."

My jaw works like Evie's, but I don't know what to say. Aunt Janet is family. But showing up now still doesn't make things right.

Aunt Janet looks at the three of us.

"That's all right, sweetie. I'm . . . I'll be staying with friends in Uptown. Just by the old McKenzies Bakery on Lyons. Here. . . ." She reaches into her purse for a pen and paper, and writes down an address.

"Come see me when you get settled. We have a lot to talk about, Kennie."

I take the paper numbly. Kennie. No one, not even G'ma, calls me that. It's a baby name, one I gave up long ago, when Mackie died. It makes me study my aunt's face really hard. I haven't seen her in thirteen years.

Miss Clare and Evie stand next to me as Aunt Janet climbs into a car across the street. It looks brand-new, and drives away just fine. I don't know what to think.

"What a liar," Evie laughs after Janet's gone.

"Merciful God, that woman's brazen," Miss Clare agrees with a shake of her head. I want to be angry, to keep them from talking like that, but a few minutes ago, I'd have agreed with them.

"Oh, I'm sorry, Kendall. I know she's your aunt, but she left me in such a fix leaving like that, and the way she left you, too . . . it makes my blood boil."

"I know," I tell her softly. "Hey, you're gonna be late for work."

"Work." Miss Clare looks around like she's forgotten her keys. She presses her fingertips to her forehead and massages a worry line.

"Right, right. I should go." She edges toward her car. "Listen, call me if you need anything. But don't let that woman into the house."

She gives Evie a quick kiss on the cheek.

"Bye, kid. Gonna make pork chops tonight."

Evie dodges the kiss unsuccessfully. She's looking at me. "You don't believe her, do you, Kendall?"

Clare and Evie both study my face. I lean up against the door frame and sigh. "The thing is, she's still family."

Neither one of them try to stop me when I leave.

25

It's not a shotgun shack, like most of the ones around here. That's the first thing I notice when I reach Janet's place. It's like our house, but it's only one unit, and it's got a front porch, whitish gray and sagging. The house used to be baby blue, I'd guess. Now it's just bruised. I can hear music inside. It's loud, like Mr. Dink's Mardi Gras party. That party seems like a thousand years ago.

The house doesn't look too friendly. And the music doesn't say "dance with me," like at the party. This is "stand back, no kids allowed" music. I open the gate and notice the beer bottles on the porch. I hesitate again. The door is open, but the screen door is shut. Someone is coming toward me from inside the house.

It's a man, but he doesn't see me. He pushes his head up against the screen and tries to look up and down the street. Whatever he's looking for isn't there. He takes a swig of beer and disappears back inside. I wonder if that's the infamous Carl.

Only one way to find out.

I knock on the frame of the door. *Family, family,* my blood beats inside my temples. I hear lighter footsteps. My pulse quickens. I'll get to see Mama's smile again.

"Hell, Jerry, I thought you said–oh. Hi! Hi, Kennie." It's Aunt Janet in the same jeans, but the sweater's gone, replaced by a man's undershirt, and a bandana covers her hair. Her voice is still sweet when she talks to me, but I get the feeling "Jerry" hasn't heard it that soft in a long long time.

Aunt Janet looks nervous for a minute, like I'm gonna jump at her and say "Boo!" or something. And then she starts to smile that Mama smile at me. If anything was suspicious about her, it melts away in that smile.

"Kennie, I'm glad you came. I knew Clare'd be mad at me, but I guess I should say my piece before you start hating me too."

She pushes past the screen door and wraps me in her arms. I'm a good three inches taller than Aunt Janet. She's so slight, I feel like I'm hugging a child. Beneath her lilac perfume, I can smell hair spray and onions. She doesn't invite me inside.

When she pulls away from me, there are tears in her eyes. Onions, I tell myself. She smells like onions. Could they be crocodile tears? "Oh, Kennie. We're all we've got left, huh? My only family."

She sounds so forlorn, for a minute I feel like we've switched places and I'm the one who's supposed to be comforting her. But then I remember who we really are.

"Why didn't you come to the funeral?" My voice is harder than I thought it would be. Aunt Janet blanches.

"Baby girl, I told you. Car trouble." I look at her hard, like I can get to the truth just by staring. It must work, because she sighs. "Carl trouble is more like it. My ex. He was supposed to take me, but Miami sounded better to both of us, to tell you the truth." She waves me toward a porch bench. We sit down and I see those years climb back onto her shoulders. Her fingers twitch like Miss Clare's, like they're looking to hold a cigarette. "Kennie, baby, there are some things you just don't understand. Mama was no friend of mine. She wouldn't have missed me at all."

"Mama . . . ," I repeat, and then I realize she means her mama, G'ma.

"Honey, we had a falling out a long time ago. Got to be that just thinking about her made me feel hurt all over again. So . . ." She smiles at me, that stolen smile. "So, better to stay away, right?"

It's a hypothetical, but I'm guessing she'd take an answer. Too bad I don't have one to give.

"What about Mama's funeral. My mama's?"

Aunt Janet's smile fades again. This time, she reaches around and does find a pack of Marlboros sitting on the windowsill behind us. She pulls a book of matches out of the pack and lights up in one comfortable movement.

"Kendall." She doesn't look at me when she speaks. "Kendall, you know what a levee does? It keeps the river from flooding the valley on the other side.

"My mother was a big old river, and I was a tiny little town. Your mama was the only thing holding her back. When Ginnie died . . ." She hangs her head and I see a tear fall onto the porch floor. Maybe they aren't onion tears after all.

"When Ginnie died, it scared me so bad, I didn't know what to do. Nothing to hold back Mama's anger, and no one left to talk to. I couldn't face Mama alone. Not with her blaming me. I tried, and I just couldn't do it."

She looks up at me, and years of sleepless nights shadow her eyes. "I was at your mama's funeral. That was the last time I saw any of you. You should know that, Kendall. Know the truth. I didn't forget the golden rule." She laughs sadly. It's my turn to look down, but Aunt Janet catches my eye anyway. "Family," she says. Family.

I swallow hard. How's this supposed to be family? No matter how much she smiles like Mama, I just can't see it.

"Why?"

"I told you why."

"No, why did G'ma blame you?"

Aunt Janet goes ashen and looks away from me. I reach into my back pocket and pull out her letter to my mother, the one that brought me to New Orleans in the first place.

"Does it have something to do with this?"

She recognizes the old letter without even touching it. Her forehead folds into such sorrow lines, she looks twenty years older. Her fingers drop before she can take the paper, cigarette burning dangerously low in her hand. Aunt Janet's eyes are on the envelope, but they're looking past it, past everything.

"Oh, Kendall." She almost sobs my name. "Your mama came down here to help me. I turned her away and she died. It was my fault. Mama was right to blame me. It was my fault."

I shake my head like movement can clear my confusion. "What do you mean, your fault? My family died in a car accident. What's that got to do with you?"

Aunt Janet buries her face in her hands, cigarette so close to her hair, I reach up and pull the burning stub away, dropping it into an ashtray. She shudders when I touch her. I kneel on the porch and peel her hands away from her face.

"Please, I want to know."

Janet looks at me for a long time, eyes swimming with regret, sorrow and pain like I've never known. She touches my cheek with a fingertip. "The little 'miracle baby of Interstate Ten.' That's what the newspapers called you."

She sighs, looks away from me, and in that motion, the tears roll out of her eyes and down her cheeks. She wipes them away as if she's ashamed.

"When I was nineteen, I was supposed to transfer to college in Chicago. I was gonna live with you, Kendall, and little Mackie. Help Ginnie around the house and go to school. It's what my mama wanted, and Ginnie thought it'd be best. They'd both left New Orleans and it worked out for them. But I thought I knew better. I found myself a place to run off to, and a man to take care of me.

"Not the best idea. And not the best man, as it turns out. Steve and I almost got married. We would've, too, if he hadn't started beating me. Cops found out, and I was so ashamed, I had to do something. So I told my big sister, asked her to come get me. I could've been in Chicago by the end of the week, back in school, back on track, like nothing had ever happened. As long as Mama didn't know the real reason why, I was willing to leave Steve behind.

"Ginnie didn't hesitate. She pulled you two out of day care, and brought your dad along to back her up. By the time she got here, though, everything had changed." Her mouth curls into a bitter smirk, and she lights another cigarette without looking at me.

"Steve had promised to clean up his act. I was already enrolled in beauty school. I figured, what the hell. I can still do this on my own."

Janet takes a deep breath, fresh cigarette burning away in her hand, lit just for comfort. She turns to me. "Your mama showed up on my doorstep expecting to find me with packed bags. And I turned her away. Just turned her away.

"She was so mad. So sorry for me. She took off out of here like hell on wheels when she saw I wouldn't change my mind. The police said she was the one driving when the car hit an ice patch out on the interstate. It gets cold down here in winter, even though we don't like to think so. Your mama was so upset. She probably never saw that ice."

She shakes her head. "For some reason, you survived. It was in the papers and everything. Ginnie's little 'miracle baby,' thrown free from the car. I thought it was a sign from God. I wanted to be back with Mama so bad. I wanted to be a family again. To take care of you.

"I'm your godmother, Kendall. Ginnie wanted us to be together. But one look from my mother over Ginnie's casket was all it took. I wasn't strong enough to stand up to that. Worst of all, because she was right."

She looks me in the eye and grips my hand with her own. "Mama never told you what happened between us to keep you away from me. And I've spent the past thirteen years avoiding you for your own good." She sighs and collects herself. "When Mama died, I saw my chance. To finally be there for you. But I couldn't do it."

She shakes her head again. "Kendall, I've been without a family for so long, I don't know what family means. Seemed like all I could do was hurt you, with the truth about your family, about me. I decided I'd rather be alone than feel ashamed again. I don't know what else to say."

She lets go of my hand and sits up straight, staring at her lap.

"I waited for you in Chicago for three days."

"I know."

"I must've left you fifteen messages."

"I heard them today."

I give an incredulous laugh. "You abandoned me."

"I know."

"Do you? Really."

She has the good grace not to answer.

"Look, I don't know why G'ma gave up on you. You're her daughter. I wouldn't have thought she had it in her." Janet's jaw tightens. "But I do know that it must have hurt her to do it. Because, when she lay there dying, she wasn't thinking about anybody but you."

I pause, choked by the memory of that hospital room, of G'ma slipping away.

"She asked for your forgiveness." I say it so softly, I wonder if Janet hears me. "She made a mistake."

Aunt Janet doesn't say anything. She just takes another drag of her cigarette. The smoke leaves her mouth in a slow, shuddering stream, up into the night sky. She looks down at her lap.

I blink back my own sorrow and clear my throat.

"So, where's this Steve guy now?"

Aunt Janet waves her hand in the air. "I left him right before Ginnie's funeral. He really was no good."

"Did you love him?"

"What?" Aunt Janet looks surprised. "No. Should I have?"

"Seems to me if you're gonna leave your family for someone, you should at least love him."

Aunt Janet laughs again, and it almost sounds like a cough. "Kennie, I didn't run away to be with some man. A man *helped* me run away from my mama. The cheapest ticket out of Wrightville. You know what my mother used to say about me? She'd say, 'Janet, you done this wrong, and that wrong. And two wrongs–' "

"Don't make a Wright," I finish for her. We both laugh, even though it feels wrong to joke around right now. Aunt Janet knew G'ma as well as I did. I wonder if she misses her as much.

"I used to tell her that's why I was a Washington."

Aunt Janet smiles. "She must've given you hell for talking back."

"Yeah, but then I'd hide her teeth and she'd get all nice again if I helped her find them."

"Shoot, girl, if she'd lost her teeth when I was seventeen, maybe I'd be a better woman today."

We both smile, and suddenly I feel an ease I haven't felt in months. I sit back up on the bench and sigh. I'm home now. I'm with family. Aunt Janet must be thinking the same thing. She looks at me and smiles.

"Hey, those friends of yours?" she asks after a minute. Marcus and Evie are waiting for me on the curb. They must have followed me. I wonder how long they've been there.

"Yeah," I say.

"Invite them up."

I stand up, feeling shy all of a sudden. "I can't, really. . . . I mean, Evie's wheelchair can't go up the stairs."

"Hmm," Aunt Janet muses. "Well, I'm sure glad you came, Kendall." She brushes a bit of wild hair down from the side of my head.

It's the end of the conversation, but I don't want it to be over.

"Will you be here for a while?" I ask.

"For a little while," Aunt Janet says. "How about you?"

"Yeah."

We stare at each other for a long moment, and I wonder if she's seeing Mama and G'ma in me the way I'm seeing them in her.

"Good." Aunt Janet gives me a hug. I hug her back like I won't let go. And then I get up from the porch, and walk away.

I come down off those steps feeling funny, like one foot's on an elevator and the other's on solid ground. Evie and Marcus have the sense not to ask me any questions. I just put my hands on Evie's chair and start to wheel her home. The air smells wet, like it's going to rain despite the sunshine, and Evie's wheels are crunchy against the chipped pavement.

Two wrongs don't make a Wright. G'ma did say that a lot, especially when I was little, every time I did something I shouldn't have done. I wanted nothing more than to be a Wright, like G'ma, like Mama. So I tried to be good. But not Aunt Janet. She did a lot of wrong things with her life, and she knows it too. I shake my head. Don't cast the first stone, Kendall. It only takes thinking of G'ma's broken grave to know I've done more than a few things wrong myself.

I catch Marcus looking at me, and smile. He smiles back, and I can see the relief drop down into his shoulders and spread to his walk. Evie sees it too, because she twists around to look up at me. The sun is bright in her eyes, but she squints and keeps looking, and finally she smiles too.

"Are you gonna tell us what happened?"

I think for a minute. "Are you gonna tell your mom you want to sing?"

Evie frowns. "That's blackmail."

I shrug. "I call it tough love."

Evie smiles. "So, we're going home?" she asks.

I push her across the street and we turn the corner before I answer.

"Yeah. We're going home."

ABOUT THE AUTHOR

Sherri L. Smith has worked in animation, film, comic books, and construction. Her first novel, *Lucy the Giant,* was named an ALA Best Book for Young Adults and a Children's Book Sense 76 Pick. She lives in Los Angeles.